HOW DO YOU WRAP A LIFE?

By Lee Walker

WHOEVER YOU ARE,

I HOPE YOU ENJOY
YOUR READ.

For Claire & Eliza.
Thanks for believing in me.
X

- ONE -

It hurt…a lot. A deep, dull ache in my chest. Pretty much how I'd expect to feel if I'd had open heart surgery. Which is an accurate description considering what had happened. Only my heart hadn't undergone a surgical operation, it had been wrenched from my chest, kicked about for a bit, stomped on, smashed against a wall like a squash ball, and then returned, battered and bruised to its original position. All without any form of anaesthetic.

So there I was, 35 years and 364 days old, and single again. The woman who was to be my wife, had brought our engagement to a premature end, having decided that it was far easier to have a close, loving relationship, if you weren't dogged by the possibility of your fiancee finding out! I referred to the woman I still loved as the Tin-man.

Nursing a broken heart and seemingly irreparable shattered dreams, I had done the only rational thing that a mature adult could, I'd run away. Which is why I found myself trying to erect a tent, on a windy, coastal campsite sometime after midnight, armed only with the front light from my, seldom used, push-bike. It wasn't my tent, so I was unfamiliar with the exact construction, but I wasn't stupid, I'd asked for instructions.

I unfolded a single sheet of A4 paper, and found a hastily scribbled diagram which resembled one of those triangular, Swiss chocolate bars. Next to this minimalist piece of art, my comedian of a best friend had drawn an arrow that pointed towards the top of the page and written the words, 'This way up'.

How hard could it be to put up a tent anyway? That's what I told myself when the wind caught the paper, whipped it out of my hand and sent it cartwheeling across the field, into the

4

darkness.

I spent a clumsy forty-five minutes, fumbling with alien material, as I tried to find and unfasten unfamiliar clips and zips, whilst cursing quietly so as not to wake anyone. It brought back memories of my first girlfriend. Only then I hadn't been holding a bike light between my teeth.

When I'd hammered in the last peg, I crept past the other tents, climbed the sand dunes, and sat myself down on the beach just beyond the high tide mark.

I'd taken the news of my transformation into a single man with unparalleled stupidity. Three hours, a couple of hundred miles, and one hasty decision later, I'd returned to the location of a family holiday some 25 years before. Simpler times when the 11-year-old me had no worries. A time when stress was defined by the lateness, or non-completion of my homework, and pain was the physical affliction that came when I fell off my bike. I was sat on the beach where, years before, I'd enjoyed splashing in the water with my younger brother, and playing ball games with my Dad.

It might have been the same beach, but without the laughter and the sunshine, it was eerie, like a wedding reception after all the guests have left. It was an open space, but the night made it feel claustrophobic. The only sound was the waves as they rushed up the sand.

When you're alone, the space around you is empty; loneliness is the empty space inside. At that moment there was a void inside and out. I had never felt lonelier in my life.

I took my phone out of my pocket and stared at the screen. I was beyond the reach of any phone signal, and I realised that I wanted to speak to her. I was sure I could persuade her to give me another chance. I could become the person she wanted to love. I just needed the opportunity to talk to her. Unfortunately it was late and, even if I'd had a network connection, there'd have been no point in calling as she'd be asleep. My heart sustained another blow, when I realised that she would have been laid in bed alongside another man.

I missed that kind of intimate moment, the romantic walks, the cuddles on the sofa, the sleeping side by side.

A single tear trickled down my cheek. I hadn't even realised I was crying. I wiped it away, but it was quickly replaced by another.

Welcome to Dumpsville: Population - Me!

I returned to the campsite and weaved my way between the handful of neighbouring tents. I was glad to see that my structure was still standing. I crawled inside; my borrowed tent was spacious. The sleeping bag was two red tea-cloths that had been sewn together, it looked inadequate, but Bestie had assured me that it was '*used by professionals*'. I can only assume that those '*professionals*' were pot-washers in a cheap restaurant.

In my rush to get away, I'd forgotten to take a pillow, so I bunched up my coat and laid my head on it. Pillows with pockets, now there's an idea to pitch to 'Dragon's Den'. I was miles from home in a place from my own past, that had no connection to our life together. It was somewhere where I should have been able to escape from all thoughts of Tin-man. I slowly sank into unconsciousness, then resurfaced when I remembered that she had been responsible for my last stay under canvas.

A completely different set of circumstances meant that I'd also been unable to sleep that night too. Her suggestion of a camping trip had me excited about the possibility of spending a romantic night alone, in the bosom of mother nature. In reality, she'd invited two of her friends and we were all crammed into a three berth tent. I was incredibly uncomfortable.

In my own bed I could squirm and fidget, until I found the perfect position. Sandwiched tightly between my girlfriend and her best friend meant that any movement sent a ripple across my fellow campers, like a human Newton's cradle. I wondered how people ever got to sleep after a threesome. What if you needed to use the toilet in the middle of the night? You were bound to wake one of them. It'd be like trying to negotiate an assault course, but the obstacles tutted and made sarcastic comments as you clambered over them. And what if they wanted to fall to sleep whilst you held them, wouldn't you lose feeling in both arms? The limb numbness would have huge implications for any journey to the toilet. Not only would you have to climb over them, you'd have to negotiate two doors, bedroom and bathroom, turn on the light, maybe even lift the toilet seat, unfasten the cord in your pyjamas…it was then that I realised that if I ever did find myself in such a position, it would be very unlikely that I'd be wearing my pyjama bottoms, let alone have bothered to fasten the cord.

In my borrowed tent, there was no jockeying for space with female sleeping companions, real or fantasy. There was only one occupant; a loser with an inability to face reality who had run miles from home, and everyone he knew. I was lying if I thought I was trying to find myself, I was actually ignoring everything else. I dragged my thoughts back to the present. I hadn't slept or relaxed since she'd given me the news. The stress and strains of my day finally took their toll and I plummeted into a deep sleep.

It was one of those mornings where everything appeared to be comprised of different shades of grey. The cloud hung low and a kind of fine drizzle succeeded in making everywhere wetter than it would have been in a monsoon. It was a miserable day, but I couldn't help thinking how strangely beautiful it all looked.

I had slept surprisingly well, and straight after waking there'd been a blissful moment where I'd forgotten where I was, and why I was there. It was an ideal moment to freeze time. Whoever and wherever I was, I didn't have a broken heart. The remembrance of my loss slowly prised its way into my waking consciousness. It brought with it the full realisation of my situation.

My heart was empty, which is exactly what my bank account would be if I didn't pull myself together. As a freelance journalist I had control over my working hours, but if I didn't work, I didn't earn. At that moment, it didn't seem so important.

Despite the efforts of the small fan heater screwed to the wall, the sub-zero temperature in the shower block remained unaltered. The shower itself did have one major bonus. It was a single cubicle and not one of those communal ones.

Sometime in my journalistic past, I had worked for a newspaper that provided showering facilities for those who cycled to work or, like me, those who would rather someone else paid for their hot water. Unfortunately they were the communal type. The three shower heads were too close together, so if the two end showers were occupied, then no one used the middle shower for fear of bumping their bare skin against another man. A complaint to the boss about the size of the shower room, met with the reply that it could comfortably accommodate three people. I had to explain that, '*comfortable*', was not an adjective I could use when I was stood next to another naked man.

I showered quickly and the campsite was coming to life as I walked back to my temporary accommodation. The flaps on the neighbouring tent opened and it gave birth to four adults. They retrieved items from the nearby car which was the same small, family type that I'd owned before my premature mid-life crisis had forced me to buy my little sports car. A move that Tin-man had disapproved of, as there was nowhere to put child seats.

I had no idea how my neighbours had managed to fit everything they needed in their little hatchback. If they were away for seven days, a daily change of the most basic of items would mean they had to carry 28 sets of underwear and 56 socks. Let's, for argument's sake, say they had packed two pairs of trousers each and as many sweaters. Even the bare minimum of clothing would be enough to fill the car to overflowing.

I decided that camping was an art form. The more you went, the more you learned to cut your luggage to the essentials. I wound the wire around the handle of my hair-dryer and dropped it into the boot.

I spent the day in a kind of daze, driving around aimlessly. I inadvertently strayed into the path of a transmitting tower, and my phone sprung into life indicating the arrival of a number of text messages. I glanced at the screen and saw they were from Tin-man. The previous night's optimism had gone, in its place was confusion and a desire never to hear from her again. The final telephone call had caused such pain that I didn't want to risk the possibility of further hurt. I was incredibly sad, but also immeasurably angry.

I couldn't bring myself to open the texts and I was still staring at the phone when it rang. Tin-man's name flashed on the screen, together with a self taken photo of both of us smiling. I looked at the picture and couldn't decide whether there was a hint of falseness in her smile. I tossed the phone over my shoulder into the back seat of the car where it continued to ring hopefully.

In answer to a prayer that I hadn't even uttered, a pub with a sea view appeared, and tempted me away from my thoughts with the promise of alcohol, so I stopped and bought a drink. I sat outside and enjoyed the rare appearance of the sun. I watched a small car ferry battle its way against the current to an island, less than a mile away. I lost interest when, after three crossings, it became apparent that the likelihood of the ferry capsizing was slim.

A large cloud squeezed the sun back behind it and uniform greyness prevailed again. I sighed heavily and closed my eyes. My brain chose that moment to project the image of her face onto the inside of my eyelids. I blinked. I didn't want to see her. I tried to think of something, anything; just to get my mind off her.

I took my phone out of my pocket to distract myself; the signal had left me again, but the messages were still there. I didn't read them, I just pressed delete. When the screen had cleared, I noticed something else…the date, it was my birthday. I silently wished myself, *'many happy returns'* and I was unable to stop my brain bursting into a melancholy version of the 'Happy Birthday' song.

Although I had put physical distance between me and the cause of my pain, I hadn't escaped my sadness. There was no way that running could erase three years of shared memories. I had to take action and that meant heading home, the procrastination was costing me money.

I finished my drink and took a walk along a path that traced the outline of the coast. The sense of my loss was immense. She was the woman I was supposed to marry. She was the one who had calmed me down and turned me into a sensible adult. I felt empty without her.

The cold wind helped push me up an incline to the top of a cliff, but when I stopped to take in the view across the sea, the wind got lazy and went straight through me. I sank further into my coat and buried my hands in the pockets. The grey water, that stretched as far as I could see, turned white as it smashed into jagged rocks way below me.

There are no rules about how long a heartbreak should last. If there were, then all I had to do was sit out the required waiting period and I would have instantly felt better. Like physical injuries, the depth of the cut determines how long it takes to heal. The cuts were still fresh and I couldn't see a time when I wouldn't hurt. I had to do something to move on.

My phone chirped and buzzed in my pocket as it reconnected with civilisation. I took it out and I watched the screen as the delayed messages came through. Every one of them from Tin-Man.

The number of texts steadily increased and with them my anger. I had made a decision, I was heading home. If I was going to get over this split then I had to start taking steps to remove her from my future, and erase her from my past. It wasn't going to be easy, but there were things to do; I had a wedding to cancel. It was over, I had to accept it.

The message counter on the phone celebrated as it reached double figures, I drew my hand back over my shoulder, and hurled the handset over the cliff and into the sea. I watched as it was swallowed by the churning waves.

- TWO -

When you rely on people contacting you to offer work, jettisoning your phone into the North Sea is a monumentally stupid move, so I forked out money I didn't have for a new handset.

Once life had been breathed into the phone, it spewed out the messages it had been holding on to. The previously unread texts from Tin-man had stubbornly refused to go away and were mixed up amongst more important, and less painful, messages. I selected the ones I didn't want to read, and deleted them.

I was left with a handful of requests to check my emails, some voice-mails telling me to check my texts, and emails telling me to check my voice-mail. Technology makes it so difficult to avoid your responsibilities.

It had taken years to build up a portfolio of newspapers and magazines who used my services, but the world of journalism is fickle. Let someone down once and you find yourself not being asked again.

I'd been back home for four days and life was getting back to normal, well if you didn't count the fact that my house and bed were empty. In the days where I'd waited to replace my phone, the enthusiasm for cancelling the wedding arrangements had waned. I couldn't face the prospect of telling people who I didn't know, that I was a loser and my fiancee had left me. It was an admission that I'd failed as a man. I was so useless at being a boyfriend, that she had found satisfaction elsewhere.

I found some solace in getting back to my day job. Tin-man would have made me sit at the dining room table to work because I made the place look untidy but, unencumbered by her rules, I flipped the laptop open and rested it on the arm of the sofa. Being self-employed means there's no health and safety killjoy to criticise my workstation or lack of correct posture.

I can't remember what feature I was working on or who it was for, but I can remember the silence. It was never a noisy house, Tin-Man didn't like racket, but as I sat on my own staring at a computer screen, it was too quiet. The damned art-deco clock she'd insisted looked classy, was tick ticking on the mantelpiece. Why couldn't it '*tick tock*' like a normal clock? Everything that woman touched was substandard.

The tick seemed to get louder. I got up and snatched the clock from its place. I prised the battery from the back and dropped them both into the bin. I looked around the room and noticed that everything was a reminder of 'us'. There wasn't a single thing that we hadn't bought together, and I could remember the moment when each one had been purchased. Getting over her wasn't going to be easy.

I grabbed a couple of photo frames that had stood either side of the clock. Where once there'd been photographs of a happy couple, I saw a jilted man and a slut. There was that smile again, I couldn't decide whether it was false or not. I resigned the frames to the same bin as the clock.

Surrounded by too many memories and insufficient bin space, I decided that the house wasn't an appropriate creative environment, I needed to find somewhere else to work. Luckily, I knew just the place. I'd once been a reporter for a provincial newspaper and when I'd become self-employed, they'd given my new career a boost by commissioning me to do articles for them. It was only local interest stuff, but they paid me per story. The paper had changed hands a couple of times and editors had come and gone. It was likely that none of the staff or bosses had remembered who had employed me and my name probably appeared in a clause on a lease. I never complained; a little bit of extra money was always useful.

The newspaper staff were all busy typing away and when I entered a few heads popped up above their monitors, like meerkats. A couple of people grunted a disappointed greeting, that suggested they were expecting someone more interesting, then bobbed back down.

"The wanderer has returned," said a voice, it was the Receptionist. She hadn't bothered looking up when I walked in and still stared at her screen. "Where have you been?" she asked.

I found a desk and sat down. "I've been away for few days."

"Ah, a romantic break in a cosy little cottage. Just the two of you snuggled up in front of a roaring log fire." The reflection of whatever she was working on, left little white squares on the lenses of her glasses.

"It was a tent."

"Oh, that's still romantic. Huddled together to keep warm, under a starry sky."

"I was on my own."

She looked at me for the first time. "She let you go away on your own?" She sounded surprised.

"Not exactly. She didn't know, and she didn't care." I turned the computer on and the monitor flickered.

"Wow, I thought you were using every spare minute to plan the wedding of the century."

"There's not going to be a wedding." She was going to find out sooner or later and I'd rather admit it now so I didn't have to field all her questions abut my non-existent relationship.

"She's left me," I said.

There was an awkward pause. "And the award for fitting her foot perfectly into her own mouth goes to…me." She pointed at herself.

I tried to laugh, but it came out as a short huff noise.

"I'm sorry." She stood up, walked over to me and leaned on the edge of the desk

"You weren't to know."

"Dare I ask why it broke down?" She hoisted herself up so she was sat on the desk.

I sighed. "Another man." I started typing and hammered the keys a little too hard.

"Really, you don't look the sort."

"Not me, her!"

"I know, I'm trying to cheer you up."

"Thanks for trying, but the wounds are still raw."

"You know what they say, when you fall off a bike you need to get straight back on it." She rapped my knuckles with her pen and I stopped typing.

"What's that supposed to mean?"

"You need to start dating again."

"Whoa! I've been single less than a week. I'm still grieving."

"And how long is that going to go on for? When you have a set back, a little bit of what caused your pain will help you get through the agony."

"Did an alcoholic tell you that?"

"No, my mum."

"Same thing."

"Cheeky." She slapped my arm and slid off the desk. "Coffee?" she asked.

"Please." I watched as she walked away towards the kitchen. The thought of finding another woman and wasting a few more of my advancing years, only to be cast aside when someone better came along, filled me with dread.

I really didn't like the idea of getting backing into the dating game. I was too old for clubbing and I didn't know what available people did to meet other available people. There was always the internet, but with my luck I'd arrange a meeting and my blind date would turn out to be a 50-year-old, fat, male serial killer.

I was just wondering if Tin-man would be upset when she discovered I'd been brutally murdered whilst I'd been on a date I'd arranged to get over her, when the Receptionist returned with two steaming mugs of coffee. She set one down on the desk and then stood over me, cradling the other in both her hands as if trying to absorb its heat. "So, what's your plan?" she asked

"I don't know. I think maybe I'll just wait a little bit longer."

"For what?"

I sat back in the chair. It was no use trying to write whilst

I was undergoing interrogation. "Well, you never know. Things change."

She rolled her eyes. "You're expecting her to come back to you, aren't you?"

"Well, she's called a few times and I've had a bundle of messages from her."

She slammed her mug down and it clinked as it collided with mine. "Did you answer the phone?"

"No."

"Did you reply to the texts?"

"No."

"Good, and you need to keep it that way."

"The calls have stopped anyway."

She grabbed the arm of the chair and swivelled the whole thing so that I faced her. She put her free hand on the other arm rest and leaned towards me. "Listen. Go home. Bag up her stuff and get rid of everything that reminds you of her."

I nodded.

"Cancelled the wedding?"

I shook my head. I felt like a naughty child being scolded by a parent.

"The honeymoon?"

I shook my head again. I was such a disappointment.

"What the hell? Why are you sat here working when there's stuff to sort?"

"I need the money."

She let go of one of the chair arms, reached across to the computer and pressed the off button. She used the same hand to point towards the door. "Go! Make some phone calls. I'll get the editor to throw a couple of assignments your way. Just do as I say."

Sheepishly, I stood up and walked the direction she had pointed.

"And don't you dare call her or answer her texts," she jabbed a finger in my direction and I left.

- THREE -

Someone once told me that the process of getting over a failed relationship was like crossing a river using stepping-stones, you had to do it one step at a time. There's something I've learned about stepping stones; first, always check the water, if it's too deep or the current too swift, then find somewhere else to cross. Second, never put your full weight on a stone until you're sure of your footing. And lastly, stepping-stones are never big enough to hold two people, you have to cross alone.

It was time I came to terms with the situation and act like the 36-year-old man that I'd unknowingly become.

Things moved quickly once I decided to act on the Receptionist's instructions. I spent a number of days making phone calls and sending emails. Most of the time I lied because I didn't want to have to explain that I'd been cuckolded. If I didn't say the words to someone else, then it couldn't be true.

I had no idea what Tin-man wanted when she had bombarded me with messages, but I guessed it had something to do with collecting her belongings from the house. I no longer wanted to see the jointly purchased household items, and her clothes neither suited or fit me, so I bagged them up. I'd been ordered not to call her, but she needed to collect her stuff, I had to remove her from my life and that meant everything that was connected with her. I suppose I could've just thrown them away, but she'd have probably reported me for theft and I'd have ended up in prison, and a good looking boy like me couldn't afford that.

By virtue of the fact I'd hurled my mobile phone into the North Sea, where it had been smashed to death by angry waves, I no longer had her number stored in a digital phone book. Unfortunately my own memory couldn't be wiped so easily. So I tapped in the number I had called so many times before. My finger hovered for a second over the green call button. I took a deep breath, and pressed it.

The second ring was interrupted by a male Geordie voice. My heart sank and cold water splashed against my insides. I heard my own voice ask to speak to her.

"She does na' wanna talk ta ya." The sentence rose in pitch as he spoke. If he'd spoken for any longer, then his words would only have registered on the hearing scale of dogs.

He was obviously acting on her instructions as I could hear her muffled voice in the background. I'll never understand women, last week she'd sent dozens of texts, and now she didn't want to talk.

I was abrupt and to the point. "Ok, but the text messages I'm getting suggest otherwise. Get her to call me if she wants her stuff back. Oh, and I could do with some help cancelling the wedding arrangements."

I stayed on the line long enough to hear a confused, guttural grunt followed by some angry mumblings, which suggested my revelation of a planned marriage was news to him. Then I hung up.

In the face of misery I felt I'd scored some sort of victory. I hadn't won the war, but I had dropped an almighty bomb, the fallout from which would hopefully be felt in their relationship for some time afterwards.

Following the call, I imagined them arguing. I always lost our arguments, most men do. It's not that we think we are wrong, it's just that women have the stamina to continue arguing long after a man has lost interest.

Part of me was glad to have thrown a cat into the aviary of their relationship, but I still felt sad. He may now be arguing, but he was arguing with the woman I loved.

Although I thought I had a whole new attitude and approach, picking the phone up to cancel the honeymoon was difficult.

The travel agent explained how they intended to fleece me for as much money as possible if I cancelled the holiday. They would then advertise it as a late availability for roughly the same price, and make more money than they would have done by just selling the holiday once. Okay, so that's not exactly what they told me, but I can read between the lines.

Apparently, the only way to avoid a cancellation charge was to actually go on the holiday. Going away on my own, on what should have been my honeymoon, was a depressing thought. The blood-sucking travel agent suggested another option. I could change the name on one of the tickets and then chose a new destination and date, I'd have a completely different holiday with another companion. There'd be administration fees of course. Now there was a surprise.

It took some doing, but I eventually managed to convince my best friend that although, it was technically my honeymoon, it was a different date and location. And we wouldn't have to share a bed. When I'd finally allayed his homophobic fears that people would think we were a couple, he agreed to accompany me.

I've known Bestie for five years, and neither of us can remember how we met, but at some stage in our past our paths crossed and we decided we liked each other enough to 'hang out', which usually involved going out every weekend where we drank too much and tried, in vain, to chat up countless women.

Despite his inability to successfully conclude any of those interactions, Bestie never shied away from initiating contact with the female of the species. On one occasion he had walked over to two girls in a bar and made his introductions. He introduced me as his visiting Australian cousin. Brilliant opening line...unless that is, you are supposed to be that cousin.

Whilst Bestie entertained one girl, I bluffed my way through Antipodean culture and geography with her friend. I spent two hours using an Australian accent I'd picked up watching late night re-runs of 'Prisoner Cell Block H'.

When the object of my deceit made one of those tandem

visits to the toilets that women always make, I seized the chance to plead with Bestie that it was about time to come clean. He said it was all going really well and urged me to keep up the pretence.

She was entranced; by the end of the night she kissed me, handed me her phone number, and told me she wanted to see me again.

Bestie and I had a heated discussion in the taxi on the way home. I, or rather my Australian alter ego, had succeeded in chatting up a stunningly attractive woman, and I was faced with a dilemma. If I called her I would have to admit my dishonesty. Bestie's award-winning idea was that I continue with the charade into the first date. I questioned where it would stop. I had visions of the confused looks my parents would give each other on my wedding day, when I uttered the words, "I do", in an Australian accent.

I didn't know what to do. I either threw the number away and resigned the experience to the back of my mind; referring to it in moments of reminiscence, or I could grasp the dingo by the tail, and admit my lies.

When I finally plucked up the courage to call her, my heartfelt admission and apology were met with a disembodied voice that told me, 'The other person has cleared the line'. That was the point in my life where I should've learned that liars never prosper.

Meeting Tin-man had changed the course of my life and put a stop to our soirees, but Bestie understood I'd settled down and it did nothing to lessen our friendship.

It should have been my honeymoon, so it was bound to be a solemn occasion, I wanted a relaxed break where I could contemplate my recent past and, although there was every chance that Bestie would get me into more difficult situations, it would at least take my mind off everything.

With a visit to the travel agent, a stroke of a pen, and the swipe of a credit card, I was faced with a holiday in a warm destination with my best friend, and not the romantic, post-wedding getaway I'd intended spending the money on.

- FOUR -

I'd planned for a holiday where I reflected on the happenings of the previous few months, and to say I wary was an understatement. I figured I'd be too preoccupied with what should have been to enjoy myself. I feared I'd probably put a damper on the whole thing, leaving Bestie regretting he had ever agreed to accompany me.

All those thoughts were resigned to the bin when, in the middle of the second week, I found myself stood in a bar without my shirt, as I drank a bottle of beer through the sock of the unknown, but similarly attired, guy next to me?

There was one plus point, the only camera we'd packed was tucked safely in the pocket of my trousers that, at that moment, were nestled around my ankles.

Just ten days before the sock-filter escapade, I was wishing I'd paid more attention to the safety briefing, when the spectacular electrical storm I watched from the window seat on the inbound flight, turned out to be directly above the runway. It should have given me some indication that this was to be no ordinary holiday, and would turn into the type of hedonism that you still discuss when you're sat in a nursing home, staring at a television with the volume cranked up to maximum.

The storm had knocked out all the power and we arrived at our hotel in complete darkness. It took two men to guide us to our room, one carried the camping light and the other the car battery that powered it. They lit two small candles, that wouldn't have looked out of place on a birthday cake, and left.

By the light of the small naked flames I saw the outline of two beds and a dressing table, but nothing else, it was too dark. The loud voices of two drunken Glaswegian women, filtered through the only window.

It was 3am, we were both tired from the journey so we fell into our respective beds. I made a mental note not to fall again, as the mattress appeared to be made of concrete.

A few hours later when I woke up, there were no voices from outside, so their owners had either gone to bed, or drank themselves to death. In the dim morning light I looked around the room. Last night's darkness had hidden nothing from me, the beds and the dressing table were the complete furnishings.

No natural light came into the room so I went to open the curtains, it was then I realised there weren't any. It was as light as it was ever going to get. The metal-grille covered window was at the end of a long alley that led to the bar.

I held the grille and looked down the narrow passageway, then back behind me. I was wondering whether I'd been arrested the previous night, and I was languishing in a foreign prison, when I heard a shrill yell from behind a door I assumed was the bathroom. This caused me further worry, after all I've seen '*Midnight Express*'.

I approached the door, which opened as I reached it. Bestie emerged and he looked slightly pale and he held the porcelain sink basin in both hands. Apparently he'd slipped on the floor, reached out and grabbed the basin which had come away from the wall. He'd managed to keep his balance, but his wasn't the only sinking feeling we were having. We were faced with the prospect of two weeks at the sister hotel of the Bangkok Hilton.

We decided to do the very un-British thing and complain, and set off to track down the hotel manager.

However much he denied it, the hotel manager was former US president George W. Bush, so the key to our demands was blackmail. He provided us with a better room, or we told the Iraqis where he'd been hiding. He pretended not to understand, but that cut no ice with me. He obviously fully understood our threats and must have been really desperate to protect his secret location, as he relented and gave us the best room in the hotel. It came with a balcony that was larger than the previous cell he'd tried to palm off on us, and had a view of the surrounding hills. It was also far enough from the bar to be out of vocal range of drunken Glaswegians. Things had started to look up.

The morning welcome meeting involved familiarisation with those important things that made up the foreign way of life; always haggle for goods, don't drink the water, and don't put tissue paper down the toilet. I conducted a quick check on the last 12 hours, and consoled myself with the thought that at least I hadn't tried to buy anything.

The 19-year-old tour representative was an introvert in an extrovert's job. He tried, without success, to sell trips and more out of pity than need, we bought one. It was for a pub-crawl the following night in a nearby town.

We spent the day wandering around and familiarising ourselves with the resort. We discovered a multitude of bars and clubs, advertising reduced drink prices, karaoke, and exotic floorshows. There were roadside stalls selling all manner of food, the aromas of which filled the air. It was a noisy, bustling attack on the senses. It was so far removed from the sedate, romantic location in which Tin-man had decided we were to spend our first few married days, and I quite liked it.

We'd been told to meet at 10PM for the pub-crawl, which was little late for men of our advancing years. As the day wore on we discussed the forthcoming event. It had been a pity-purchase made to help out Tour-rep. Neither of us were looking forward to it. What if it was full of couples? What if all the other pub-crawlers where boring or even worse, younger than]
us?

There was only one thing for it, we hid in a bar across the road from the meeting point and watched as the others boarded the bus. Each member was carefully scrutinised and our worst fears were recognised, they were all aged in their early twenties, and better looking.

"I've an idea," said Bestie. Most of my problems started with those words, so I can be forgiven for the twinge of apprehension that inserted itself into my conscious.

"We should catch the local bus and travel to the town and try to find the pub-crawl," he said.

As ideas went, it was one of his better ones so a 15-minute rickety bus ride later, we were hunting around the neighbouring town for a group of people with which we had no intention of spending any time. It may have been luck, judgment, or just the fact that we tried all the bars in town, but we found them and we watched from a distance.

We were glad we hadn't joined in. The event had all the eloquent trappings of an 18-30 holiday. The DJ invited all the men in the group onto the stage, and we said a silent prayer as they were instructed to strip to the waist and dance provocatively to a seventies disco hit.

We were two days into our holiday and the last thing I wanted to do was display my pasty white skin, and shake my ever-increasing waistline in front of a group of younger, better looking strangers. I'm sure people had been deported for that sort of thing.

We sacrificed a few more beers to the Great God of foresight and then left, secure in the knowledge that we had saved ourselves from severe humiliation and a possible, "*And finally...*" spot on '*News at Ten*'.

We decided to stay with the more sedate tourist trips. Unfortunately we hadn't counted on Tour-rep. Awkward and shy he may have been, but he was tenacious and possessed the kind of tracking skills only usually found in an airport sniffer dog.

It apparently wasn't enough that he'd had sold the trip and been paid for it. He still wanted the pleasure of our company. I secretly suspected that it wasn't our companionship he wanted, just the commission.

It seemed that every time I turned around he was there with his nervous smile. "So what about next week's crawl boys?" he'd ask. Each time we made our excuses and a quick exit.

We ventured out of the resort on several occasions, not just to sightsee but because it seemed the only way that we could avoid the person who had become the most irritating and omnipresent man on the planet.

A whole week passed and we became wise to Tour-rep's movements. We could predict his arrival and avoid him. He still caught us on the odd occasion. He'd appear from behind bushes or materialise suddenly in a shop, like a character from '*Mr Benn*'.

A full day boat trip offered the perfect chance to spend a day without worrying where Tour-rep would appear next. Although I would not have put it past him to have suddenly surfaced in the middle of nowhere in full scuba gear, a waterproof receipt book clutched in his hand.

As we waited to climb on board the boat, we were ordered to remove our shoes. They were all placed into a large box and hauled away along the jetty. They would be held to ransom until we paid our bar bill. It is very difficult to run across hot sand in bare feet, and if you managed to make it across the sand, once you hit the pavement your feet would melt to the concrete.

Bestie headed straight up to the sundeck and I followed. There was no shade there, so I lathered myself in the highest factor suncream available from the pharmacy. I couldn't go any further up the UV protection scale, without applying wood varnish.

Through my exposure to the sun I had started to get a bit of a tan. Well I looked like I'd been rubbed down with a wet tea-bag, but nevertheless it was a tan. I thought a few more rays would turn me into a bronzed Adonis. Actually only drastic reconstructive surgery would have made me look like anything other than a cinnamon flavoured '*Pilsbury Dough-Boy*'.

Two German girls unpacked a couple of towels each and sat alongside us, they had arrived equipped for total sun-bed domination. They undressed down to their dental floss bikinis, tucked their armpit hair discreetly away, and spread themselves out; other than to turn themselves over, they didn't move for the entire trip.

The boat spluttered away from shore and the music started. As it pitched and rolled its way out across the sea we were treated to the milk-curdling yodels of Celine Dion. I don't like to appear fatalistic in any way, but the last thing I want to hear when I'm on a boat in the middle of the ocean is the theme tune to '*Titanic*'.

There were 22 chattering seafarers on the boat, the music was a notch too loud, the motor whined away, and the sea was littered with other almost identical boats, but all I could hear was the slap of the water, the whoosh of the wind, and the flap of the flag.

Way before the land became a black line on the horizon, Bestie was snoring gently. While others sunbathed, I spent my time just looking at the water.

Could I return from this holiday being completely cured of my Tin-man induced depressions? Probably not, we'd been together too long for me to recover so quickly. The sense of loss was still very strong. I couldn't escape the fact that this was my honeymoon, and I was spending it with the oil-covered, forty-something man who was snoring just a few feet away from me.

I wondered whether I would ever speak to her again, or just hear her voice. We needed some sort of communication, she'd left clothes and shoes at the house. Everything would probably be done through an intermediary or a solicitor. Jesus! It was like she'd died and I was trying to sort out her estate, whilst I still grieved. Only she wasn't dead; she was alive and well, and living her life with a completely different man. That hurt.

I watched the blue water and small slivers of sunlight were momentarily caught in the swells and then released. I was still thinking about Tin-Man and my attention was focused on nothing in particular when, 20 metres in front of me, the water erupted. Two dolphins, sleek and smooth like polished wood, launched themselves high into the air side by side. They hung there for a split second then dropped back into the water. They left only ripples and a memory behind. Some of my fellow day-trippers had heard the noise, but no-one else had seen them, I turned to say something, but stopped. It was my moment; I was the only person on the planet to have witnessed it. I selfishly didn't want to share this experience. I felt privileged and, as if they knew their job was done, the dolphins never resurfaced.

At the end of the day, we idled back into the small port and the mooring ropes were secured. I saw two men as they hurried along the jetty, the box of ransom shoes carried between them. I was hit by the sudden thought that if I got off first, I could probably leave with a better pair of shoes than the ones I'd been wearing when I'd arrived.

Unfortunately my struggle to get off first failed miserably and I found myself stood on the jetty looking at the only pair of shoes left, mine. I was insulted that no-one had bothered to steal them.

On the day of the next pub-crawl we made meticulous plans that included ensuring we were safely locked in our hotel room, by the time of Tour-rep's scheduled hotel visit. We knew he would try our room, and hoped that when he knocked on the door and received no reply, he'd just leave.

When the time came, he hammered on the door several times and we sat frozen, in silence. He shouted our names, but still we didn't move. When he moved away from the door, it looked like our plan had worked. Then he returned and I heard him speaking to someone, there was no mistaking the voice, it was George W.

"Dare defneetly in dare," I heard him say, "I seed dem early."

Bastard! Now he's bilingual. If we just stayed quiet surely he'd leave.

"I av key."

There was a jangle of metal and I imagined George W. proudly presenting his master key. We shared a panicked look, but both had the same idea at the same time. I dived into bed and Bestie ran to the door, he messed up his bed sheets on his way across the room. He really was a stickler for the finer details.

He opened the door as George W. was about to put his shiny key into the lock.

"We were asleep," Bestie said, by way of explanation.

Without waiting for an invite, Tour-rep walked straight into the room, behind him George W. smiled and walked away.

"So boys, tonight's the night then?" I was old enough to be his father and Bestie was almost old enough to be mine, but he still insisted on calling us "boys".

It was a tense moment. Plan 'A' involved not answering the door and was so cunning and foolproof, we hadn't bothered developing a plan 'B'.

Tour-Rep sat down on one of the beds and made himself comfortable. My brain wouldn't work fast enough, there was no getting out of this situation. It was a good job that at least one of us hadn't frozen.

"What time does the bus leave?" asked Bestie.

"Ten," replied Tour-rep.

Bestie looked at his watch. "Well that doesn't give us much time to get showered and get some dinner. How about you tell us where you'll be and we'll meet you there?"

Tour-rep ripped a piece of headed notepaper off the pad he carried and wrote down the itinerary for the evening. He then produced his receipt book. This seemed to be Bestie's way to get rid of him and it was costing me another five pounds. I didn't have time to weigh up whether it was worth it before I handed over my money.

"See you later boys," he called as he left the room. He waved his receipt book, the two five pound notes fluttered mockingly from between the pages.

"Another fiver down the drain," I said as I dropped back on the bed and closed my eyes.

"Not exactly," said Bestie, "we can still go, but we can turn up when we like, all we do is..."

I sat up and finished his sentence, "...turn up at the bar after the one where we have to take our shirts off."

Brilliant!

Later that evening, as we clambered aboard the public bus, we felt confident that the pub-crawl would be well under way, and the male members would be mounting the stage, unaware that they were about to perform an Errol Brown classic, whilst semi-naked.

Our timing was impeccable; we arrived at the next bar on the itinerary just as the other members of the crawl entered. This was perfect, we arrived fashionably late without it looking like we had tried to avoid any humiliation. There was some catching up to do in the alcohol department, but we had never before shied away from a challenge.

A quick burst of group karaoke confirmed my suspicion about the age of our drinking companions. When only Bestie and I knew the words to some of the '*oldies*', our newly found friends looked to us for help; none of them had been born at the time of the original releases. Age-wise I was so out of my depth.

There were lots of silly games which involved drinking alcohol in order to win more alcohol. During the, '*Drink-tequila-off-the-body-of-a-female-you've-never-met*' experience, we both attracted the attentions of the females who had acted as our drink-holders, and they stayed with us.

My hanger-on was average in the looks department, but she probably felt the same about me…I hoped. I was slightly put off by her droning Brummie accent but not enough to ignore her attention. Unfortunately Bestie had been adopted by a Hippo-croco-pig. She was over-weight, had large thick lensed glasses, and her pock-marked skin glowed pink from prolonged, unprotected exposure to the sun.

It was the first time since my break-up that I'd had any attention from a woman and I wasn't about to ignore it, although in some bizarre way it felt like I was cheating on my ex-fiancee, but maybe the Receptionist was right, I needed to get back into the dating game.

The Brummie had volunteered me for the game where I'd being drinking beer through someone else's sock. The irony of being stood half naked in a bar full of people, when I'd tried to avoid that very situation, didn't escape me, but I was very drunk and probably thought my carefree attitude would impress her.

I redressed and as the night wore on I forgot my problems, my inhibitions, but more importantly, the last bus home. Thankfully I was not alone. Bestie had remained by my side, as had our two groupies.

It was 3.30AM and we managed to find a taxi. Bestie said he was tired and he wanted to go back to the hotel, but Brummie and I had decided that as soon as the taxi stopped, we would find a bar and continue drinking. The wheels hadn't even stopped turning when the two of us were out and running up the street, leaving Bestie and the HCP behind.

The rest of our night involved more bars, more alcohol, and some dancing.

Then I found myself back in Brummie's hotel room. There had been no suggestion that the night would end up this way. The only time our lips had met was during the Tequila drinking competition. I had enjoyed a good, fun night, and any thoughts of sexual experimentation had been light years from my mind. Mentally I was ill-prepared for a one night stand, physically I was drunk and I couldn't even raise a smile.

In the back of my mind a thought blossomed that it was wrong, or at least it had the potential to be wrong, if the situation was headed where I thought it was headed. Seeing as I now found myself in the hotel room of a female I had met only a few hours before, and we were both drunk, I couldn't be criticised for jumping to the wrong conclusion.

We sat on the edge of the bed, there was awkward conversation where previously there had been laughter and banter. There were hesitant physical approaches, where earlier there had been piggy-backs and arm linking.

I have always prided myself on my principles, my ingrained values and ethical standards. I am first to condemn those with relaxed attitudes to sex, and the care-free abandon with which they jump from bed to bed and partner to partner. I couldn't go against those beliefs, could I?

I was still desperately wrestling with my moral dilemma when someone knocked on the door.

There was a short pause before Brummie shouted, "Ullo?"

The owner of the knock replied, "'Allo, to speak with you please?"

"Oh God, it's the manager," she hissed. "Quick hide."

The room comprised of two single beds and a wardrobe, it wouldn't have taken the World hide 'n' seek champion to find me. I was contemplating my options when Brummie jumped up from the bed and pushed me so hard that I fell backwards between the bed and the patio window. I landed with a slap on the tiled floor, thankfully out of sight of the doorway.

The door opened and a voice said, "You av man in your room?"

Brummie denied it and stepped out into the hallway closing the door behind her. I heard muffled voices and consoled myself with the fact they both had accents that were too strong to translate, even if I could hear what was being said.

A few moments passed before the door opened, Brummie stepped back in and locked it behind her. "He doesn't believe me, but he's gone."

I clambered back up onto the bed and we continued our unnatural conversation, any headway we had been making towards our final destination had been lost, and we tried to regain our momentum.

We stumbled our way through a few more bits of conversation. I couldn't escape the feeling that I was about to be unfaithful to the woman who had been unfaithful to me. There was nothing connecting us any more, only memories, but this felt wrong. There was no doubt that Tin-man would have slept with her new boyfriend, so why did I feel so reticent. I was trying to change my mindset when there was another knock at the door. "It's me," whispered a female voice.

As she jumped up again the Brummie pushed me towards my hiding place. I got the hint and I laid down again between the window and bed.

I heard the door creak as it opened.

"Just wanted to check you got back ok," said a voice.

"Yeah, no problems."

"I thought you might have pulled one of the old blokes and gone back to their hotel," said the voice with a laugh.

Ah, so she'd been trying to hit on someone else before she finally landed me. Had I in fact swooped in at the last moment and saved her from making a terrible mistake with some "old bloke"?

Hold on! "old bloke" did she mean?…My thoughts were interrupted by the click of the door latch and the clunk of the lock.

I peeped over the top of the bed.

She shrugged. "It gets busy round here at night. Now, where were we?"

I pulled myself up and sat back on the bed.

Taking advantage of the silence between us I studied her and took stock of the situation. I was miles from home, in the hotel room of a female I was never likely to see again after the end of this week. She was young, slim, not unattractive, and single and I was…well I was single at least. I shuffled closer to her, and had just flicked the morality over-ride switch when there was yet another knock at the door.

I grabbed her hand as it came towards me, "I know," I said, "on the floor."

This time the door opened and there was no conversation in the hallway, whoever it was walked straight in and the noise of creaking springs told me they'd sat down on the other bed.

"I've just slept with the Tour Rep and it was crap!" said the angry female voice. "It was awful, he's got no technique, he was lacking in the equipment department, and it lasted seconds."

"I could've told you that," said the Brummie.

I almost sat bolt upright, but that would have given my position away, so I settled for a wide-eyed stare with jaw slightly agape, whilst remaining horizontal.

What followed was, if you'll excuse the pun, a blow by blow account of the sexual encounter. Poor old Tour-rep had failed to impress with either his effort or achievement. The tracking skills he practiced when looking for holidaymakers who were

tried to avoid him, apparently hadn't helped him locate a clit-
oris.

His physique was mediocre and she had tried not to laugh
when he removed his shorts. The whole experience had made
her feel nauseous, but she was on holiday and this sort of thing
was expected, and boy would she have a story to tell when she
got home.

The whole story took about 20 minutes which, I reckoned,
was about ten times longer than the actual act itself.

Throughout this 'XXX'-rated version of Jackanory, the
Brummie added her own comments. The odd, "I know", sometimes , "He didn't", and on three occasions, I counted them, she
actually said, "He did that with me too."

The marble floor had made my body numb and the insight
into the female persona had done the same to my brain. If I went
through with this, I would end up another notch on her sun-
bed, the object of ridicule in some sordid girlie conversation.
My physical appearance would be torn to shreds and my sexual technique would be critiqued and ridiculed. There was no
doubt, she would tell her friends. I would probably never meet
them so that wasn't a problem, and they never seem to share
their thoughts with other men, so my reputation might stay intact with the male population. Although you never know who
might be laid down at the side of her bed next time!

Their conversation came to an end. The bed-springs heaved
a sigh of relief as whoever it was stood up. Their voices became
muffled as they both stepped out into the corridor and closed
the door behind them.

There was nothing else for it, I had to make a tactical with-
drawal. I decided I would act like a man. I'd explain my thoughts
and reservations. I would detail my moral dilemma, and above
all I would do it with dignity and decorum.

I stood up, took a deep breath. In a sudden attack of coward-
ice I slid open the patio door, climbed over the balcony, lowered
myself the few feet into the gardens below, then I ran like hell.

When I was clear of the hotel grounds, I stopped at a shop and went inside. It was early but I bought a six-pack of beer. As the sun was rising, I sat on the kerbside outside the shop and opened a bottle. I tried to decide whether I had won a moral victory, had a close shave, or been monumentally stupid. It was probably a combination of all three.

The shop owner sat down beside me and offered me a cigarette, I shook my head but felt it only right to return his kindness. I offered him one of the bottles of the beer that, until two minutes before, he had owned. He accepted.

There I stayed for about an hour. I talked and drank beer with the owner. His English was very poor, but, after all the alcohol, I'm pretty sure mine wasn't too good either. Eventually I bid the man goodbye and headed for my hotel.

I was on the receiving end of a disapproving look from George W. when I walked back into the hotel. I didn't understand why. Despite my extra beers with the shopkeeper I was, by that stage sobering up, I was fully clothed, and I was back in time for the garbage he tried to pass off as breakfast. I then realised that I had probably been caught on CCTV going into the other hotel, copies had been made and distributed amongst hoteliers.

There was no towel on the outside door handle when I reached our room; the pre-agreed, *'Do not disturb cos I've pulled'* sign was not there. I was glad because it meant I was able to climb into my bed straightaway.

Bestie woke me at 10AM to tell me he was headed to the beach and to join him later. "Find me a lounger with some shade," I said, and then I turned over and went back to sleep for a few more hours.

I seemed to have been walking along the beach for ages, past rows and rows of empty sun-loungers but no Bestie. It was not busy and I couldn't understand where he had gone. I had just about given up when I saw him laid in the full ferocity of the sun, reading a book, not an inch of shade within 20 feet of him. I dropped myself down onto the neighbouring lounger. He ignored my greeting and didn't even look up from his book.

A few minutes passed and he hadn't turned a page. Oh my God! He'd died. I was going to have to find the British Embassy and make arrangements to have his body flown back. There would be some sort of inquest. I'd have to give evidence through a foreign lawyer, which would be horribly mis-translated and I'd spend time in a prison before being tried for his murder. Then once I'd been found guilty there'd be the embarrassment of an extradition battle with England. I'd eventually land at Heathrow to be met by thousands of paparazzi. I'd have to walk through the terminal with my jacket over my head, which posed another problem; I hadn't packed a jacket because it was going to be hot, so...

He coughed and did a double take when he realised I was there. He smiled and faced forward again. The open book rested on his bare chest, I could see it had been there some time as his suntan oil had soaked into the bottom of the pages.

"Did you have to choose a place without any shade?" I asked.

He smiled and nodded.

"You know I can't sit out in direct sunlight, I burn."

He raised his eyebrows and nodded again.

"You had the pick of all these sun beds and you chose this one. Why?"

He just nodded.

I was about to lose my temper when I realised he wasn't being ignorant, his actions were a covert indication. I followed the direction of his nod. The beach was almost empty apart from two sun-beds six feet in front of him, occupied by two top-less women who were laid on their backs. Okay, so it wasn't sun-tan oil on the pages, I really hoped it was his saliva.

There was little more I could do but sit with him and enjoy the view.

The admiration wore off when both women turned over to toast the other side. Bestie lowered his book and said, "Well, what happened?"

I thought about regaling him with the tale of my sexual con-quest, practically impossible positions I had achieved, and the depths of depravity to which I'd plunged during a night of un-bridled lust.

"Nothing," I said. "What about you? You and the Hippo-croco-pig seemed to be getting on well, what happened?"

"Well," he turned onto his side, propped his head on his hand in a casual way and continued, "you jumped out of the taxi without settling the bill, leaving me with the gargoyle whilst you disappeared on a quest for more beer. I paid the driver and we got out. I then started to head back to the hotel. The gargoyle wanted to know where I was going and I told her. She started to moan that I couldn't abandon a 17-year-old girl in the middle of a foreign town that she had only been in for a day. I tried to help, but she couldn't remember the name of her hotel. A woman this ugly shouldn't really be allowed out of her own country, but when she's stupid as well, she shouldn't be allowed out of the house.

"I tried to get her to ask at one of the bars or shops, but she became really distressed, saying she was scared, and she was on her own, and that I had to help her…and blah, blah, blah. Any-way, then she started crying."

"Oh God! What did you do?" I asked.

"Well I did the only thing I could for a distressed female who was lost and crying, miles from home."

"Which was?" I said.

"I asked her for half the taxi fare and fucked off."

- FIVE -

Tin-Man hadn't been far from my thoughts during my holiday. Any ideas I had about having magically forgotten about her in the space of two weeks were wrong. Although she wasn't constantly on my mind, I randomly thought about her and it made me catch my breath.

I'd been back from holiday a couple of weeks, and had fallen into the routine of a single man. Which, to my mum, meant I didn't have the ability to look after myself. She called to schedule a visit; she'd want to see that I wasn't wallowing in a pit of despair. She'd check up on the tidiness of my house. I would be subjected to lectures on washing, ironing, and cleaning.

Scheduled visits were the best type because it gave me time to put my affairs in order. A clean, tidy house would allay some of her fears that I might be sitting in my own filth surrounded by empty beer cans.

She also worried whether I was eating properly. She would open a kitchen cupboard and examine the contents, give a sharp intake of breath, before tutting loudly.

I looked in the fridge, it was apparent that my mother would not be the only one with concerns; it was possible environmental health would want to get involved. In an attempt to make my mother think that I lived on more than wine and takeaways, I paid a visit to the supermarket.

Trolleys are like little cars and their inconsiderate usage often leads to aisle-rage. It was my eighth head on collision with an oncoming trolley. I prepared my best frown and looked up. My irritated expression was met with a dazzling smile.

"Hello," said its owner.

My harsh expression melted and my face flushed. I recognised her immediately from my late teenage years. Whenever I went out with friends at the weekend she'd be in the same bars, surrounded by adoring men. I think we had a mutual acquaintance, I'd probably only spoken to her once.

I'd been too intimidated to ask her out on a date. She was gorgeous and any such offer would, without doubt, have been met with rejection. But I thought about her…a lot. This was the first time I had seen her in years.

"Sorry," I mumbled and negotiated my way around her.

She put her hand out and stopped me as I passed by, "You don't recognise me do you?"

My heart skipped a beat, she either remembered me, or she'd mistaken me for someone else. I paused and then feigned sudden recognition.

There followed a conversation, which contained approximately 1,000 more words than I'd ever spoken to her previously. We became the sort of customers who block access to shelves when their shopping trip turns into a social event.

I discovered that she remembered my name, the car I had driven, and where I used to live.

Although I didn't admit it, I remembered exactly the same details about her…and more. She was a Scorpio, a socialist, and a vegan. She had a passion for animal welfare and all matters environmental. She truly was 'Right-on'.

She nodded towards my trolley. "That looks healthy," she said.

Due to my unique way of shopping, and the fact that I was pending a visit from my mum, my trolley contained a large amount of fruit and vegetables, and a few bottles of expensive wine.

Some part of my brain bypassed the common sense filter, and I suddenly heard myself declare, "Yes, I'm a vegetarian."

Although made with the best of intentions, this comment was monumentally absurd. I couldn't be much further from being a vegetarian. I always bought vegetables when I went shopping, but when I took them home I never used them. My fridge had become the kind of place that provided 'end of life care' for green things. I never ate vegetables unless they'd been chipped and deep fried.

My brain had decided that she'd be more interested if we had some common ground. I silently kicked myself and I was still reeling in self admonishment, when I heard the words, "Do you fancy a drink sometime?"

Perhaps I should give in to my stupidity more often.

We exchanged numbers and parted. Going our separate ways meant I would have to complete my shopping. This would be fine until I reached the meat produce. I was likely to bump into her again at the checkout and my deceit would be revealed.

To maintain my illusion I continued shopping. I also saw Right-on a few more times. I didn't need anything as I'd already stocked up, but I threw a few more green bits into the trolley so I didn't raise her suspicions. I knew I wouldn't eat half the items and I couldn't identify the other half. It didn't matter, I would take them home and they would all pass away peacefully in the cooler drawer, somewhere between the beer and the carnivore shelves.

Despite attempts to slow down and lose her, we ended up at checkouts next to each other. We paid and loaded our shopping at the same time. There was small talk as we walked to the car park together. We said our goodbyes, promised to call, and went to our respective cars.

I lifted all my shopping into the boot and watched as she did the same. I planned to wait until she had driven out, then I would return to the store and stock up on food I would actually eat.

I climbed into the driver's seat and watched Right-on as she did the same. Whilst I waited for her to leave, I tried some delaying tactics; checking my mirrors, adjusting my seat, opening and closing the glove compartment a few times. When I next looked up she was talking into her mobile phone. There was nothing for it, if I didn't want to look like a stalker I had to leave now. I drove towards the exit and as I passed her car she gave me a smile and a little wave, while she continued to talk on the phone.

I went home with enough fruit and vegetables to stock a farmer's market. The only thing in my boot fit for consumption was wine.

I waited a whole day before making the call to arrange our date. I'd would've called sooner but I was busy doing the rest of my shopping. We agreed to go for a meal a few days later.

She was a vegan so this needed meticulous planning. I checked all my clothes for any signs of animal products. It didn't look good, I was left with a pair of jeans, a yellow cotton t-shirt, and some trainers. I wasn't sure about the trainers as I couldn't remember whether rubber came from an animal.

My aftershave didn't pass the test either, in fact the only test it had ever passed was the one on the animal who had tried it first.

I replaced some of my wardrobe with more eco-friendly items, and my aftershave with something that wasn't going to make animals eye me with suspicion. It ended up costing me a small fortune, but hopefully it was going to be worth it. You have to speculate to copulate.

On the night of the date, I was prepared. I re-checked all the labels on my clothes. I did some research and discovered that rubber comes from a tree, but I had brought a pair of man-made shoes anyway as I was slightly worried that she was just as passionate about plant welfare. While on the subject of rubber, I retrieved a condom from the redundant box in the bathroom cabinet. I pushed it into my pocket, It needed to be hidden from view when I took out my wallet, I didn't want her to think I was being presumptuous.

Dressed in my new clothes and washed and scrubbed to within an inch of my life, I gave myself the once over. I didn't own a full-length mirror so I had to stand well back from the shaving mirror. If the non-animal tested deodorant held out long enough, I might be in with a chance.

Out on the drive my pride and joy sparkled with the several

coats of wax I had lavished on it. I had checked with the sales assistant that it wasn't made from real turtles. Sitting in the driver's seat I inhaled that clean car smell. Polish and...leather! To late to disguise it now, and there was no time to buy a new car, I had to risk it.

I decided that 10 minutes was early, but not enough that I appeared over eager. When I knocked, the door opened and her face peered round it. Her dark, silken hair slightly covered her face until she brushed it back behind her ears. She smiled a sparkling smile and some of that shine entered her eyes.

My luck had changed, I was sure of it. There I was on the precipice of a new relationship with the unattainable woman of my teenage years. It was the stuff my dreams had been made of... mainly the wet ones.

"Come in," she called and she pointed to a door as she walked down the dark hallway. "Grab a seat in the living room. I'll be with you in a sec."

I pushed open the door she'd indicated. Behind it was a small room made to look even smaller by the fact that all four walls were painted in a dark shade of red. The daylight fought hard to make an impact. There were two sofas, a book case, and an intricately-carved coffee table. The wooden floor was partially covered in a rug, that had obviously been hand-woven by some little old lady in a Third World village.

It was clean and tidy. Several anti-vivisection magazines were scattered on the little table. I picked one up and flicked through it. There were lots of pictures of animals at various stages of medical testing. Beagles with upturned colanders on their heads, shaven mice with human ears grafted onto their backs, and my personal favourite, the cigarette smoking monkey.

Maybe the monkey wasn't part of the experiments. He could have been part of the staff and was just on his lunch break. I bet if the camera panned back, he'd be holding a hand of cards, surrounded by other staff, whilst he enjoyed a well earned rest.

I was allowing myself a slight chuckle when Right-on appeared in the door way.

"Something funny?" she asked.

I looked up. "Why is mankind so cruel to animals," I said, shaking the magazine.

"You mean human-kind."

"Yes, human-kind."

Part of my brain was congratulating itself on the quick thinking, another part was wondering why she'd corrected me, but the biggest part was registering what I was seeing. The face of an angel peered over the top of a knitted, rusty brown, turtle-necked sweater which reached down beyond her hips almost to the middle of her thighs. It couldn't have been wool, that would have been wrong, unless it was discarded wool collected from hedgerows by impoverished Peruvian grandmothers. Some-where beneath the sweater was the start of a bottle green skirt which flared out until it finished just short of the floor.

I'm a man, and we admire curves on a woman, but she might as well have been wearing a duvet cover. There was one bump and curve at the front of her waist that, I discovered later, was a bum bag.

"You look nice," I said.

She smiled and my heart skipped. I instantly chastised my-self for my chauvinistic thoughts. Beauty is only skin deep, it's what is underneath that's important...only I couldn't see what was underneath.

We both climbed into the car and she hesitated slightly, gave the seats a suspicious look, but didn't say anything.

As with all first dates, it started a little strained and the con-versation slightly false. There were general pleasantries until we reached the restaurant.

I locked the car and Right-on walked ahead a few feet. As she climbed the steps to the main entrance, I could swear I saw some bare ankle, but it could have been wishful thinking.

Other than our first date, and other people's birthdays, Tin-man and I had never visited restaurants. She said they were over-rated and expensive. We stayed at home and I usually cooked, which meant my knowledge of places to eat was limited. I'd sought advice from the Receptionist and she suggested one that had a good reputation and reasonable prices.

It was a simple restaurant, but unfortunately the staff were under the impression that they worked for some prestigious London establishment. Some of the waistcoat-wearing waiters looked down their noses as Right-on walked in. Ok, it was a warm night and she was showing less flesh than a shy ninja, but there was no need for the disapproving looks.

It was warm in the restaurant, and I could only imagine how hot she must have felt under all that clothing. Was she embarrassed about her body? Maybe she was hiding an extra leg or, if I was really lucky, an extra breast. Perhaps if I could persuade her to have an extremely hot curry, she would be forced to remove the jumper.

We were seated at a table and the waiter took our drinks order. She asked for a small white wine and, to be safe, I asked for mineral water. We hadn't even started the meal and she was on the alcohol. Wine versus mineral water; I was one - nil up in the sobriety stakes. If she kept it up I wouldn't need the help of a hot curry.

A different waiter reappeared at the side of the table. "May I take your order?" he asked.

I pointed to the menu. "The prawn cocktail…" I realised my mistake when Right-on looked at me through knitted eyebrows, "…does it contain real prawns?"

The waiter stared in disbelief, "Sir, by definition a prawn cocktail does contain prawns."

"Oh, I just wondered whether there was a version without the prawns." I smiled weakly.

"Then that would be a cocktail, sir."

I had to settle for melon, which really turns the meal on its head. How can a piece of fruit be a starter?

"And your main course sir? Perhaps the chicken chasseur without the chicken?" He looked at me, and raised his eyebrows.

I ignored his sarcasm and studied the menu. The unappetising vegetarian meals were all marked with a 'V'. I really wanted a steak, I should come clean now and if she didn't like it then tough. I didn't need to lie and pretend to be something I wasn't just to impress a woman. She either liked me because I was me, or she didn't like me at all. I couldn't continue with the façade. Why should I compromise my own values just to get someone to like me?

At that precise moment, she grabbed the hem of her jumper and pulled it over her head to reveal a tight-fitting white vest top, which clung to the most perfect pair of breasts imaginable.

"Vegetable curry please," I said.

The conversation got a little easier during the meal

"Are you still working as a journalist?" she asked.

"Yes, but I've been freelance for a few years now."

"Who do you work for?"

"Mostly local newspapers, sometimes the nationals, and I get commissioned to write articles for magazines?"

"I hope it's not the sort of magazines that objectify women."

It was, but the phrasing of her question meant I didn't feel able to admit it. "No, they're general interest magazines, DIY, cars, that sort of stuff." I knew nothing about either area. It was time for a subject change.

"What about you? What do you do?"

"I work for an animal charity, mostly admin and promotions. I'm responsible for spreading the word about the ethical treatment of animals."

I pictured her stood in a busy city street, shaking a donation tin, surrounded by posters of mutilated animals.

"You must see the black side of the human soul." I'd nailed it. No use of the word "man" in that sentence.

"Dark," she said.

"Yes, I'll bet it is."

"No, dark. Using the word 'black' gives it negative connotations."

Damn, just when I thought I'd figured out the rules to this

stuff.

I feigned interest and asked lots of questions. I don't remember most of the answers, because my mind kept wandering to the white top, and I found myself wondering how I could get her to remove the skirt, short of setting fire to it.

It was noticeable that the waiters were paying us more attention since the big reveal, when I say us, I mean my date, or rather her breasts.

The more she drank the more she talked. Mostly about the environment, her efforts to save it, and man's vile treatment of his fellow creatures. Ok, not "man", "human".

The rest of the meal went off without incident. She was fitted with an automatic rectifier, and if any sentence contained a politically incorrect statement, she would amend it without even interrupting the flow of conversation. It made me wonder whether she was actually listening to the content of what I said, rather than individual words. I did let slip with a couple of statements that were quickly corrected. The restaurant had 'staffing issues' not 'manpower problems', and the waiter was a person of 'alternative sexuality", and not how I had described him after his sarcastic remarks

Eventually I was scanning each sentence before I let it loose. This led to the kind of satellite delay that's usually seen in foreign news reports. She either didn't seem to notice, or thought I was retarded…sorry, 'had specific learning requirements'.

At the end of the meal I paid the bill. Her quest for equality obviously didn't stretch to going '*Dutch*'. We stepped outside and she slipped her jumper back on. She shook her hair out, slid her arm through mine, and we walked back to the car.

Outside her house, I walked her up the small path to the front door.

"I'd ask you in for coffee, but I've got work tomorrow morning and I really need to get some sleep."

I had optimistically armed myself with a condom and was a little disappointed, but I hadn't really expected the date to end in sex. She was a woman with her own set of principles, which probably included not taking a man to bed on the first date. Whether she was being truthful about the need for an early night, or was just letting me down gently, there was only one way to deal with it. "No problem," I said. "I wouldn't want us to end up in an awkward position."

Actually any position would have been good, awkward or just straight missionary, I didn't really care.

I needed to play it carefully and be the perfect gentleman. I leaned forward and kissed her on the cheek. She'd set the tone, there'd be no jumping straight into a physical relationship.

"I've had a lovely evening," she said, "you will call me won't you?"

"Of course I will," I promised. I kissed her again and walked away down the path.

I reached the car and looked back, she smiled and then turned, and disappeared inside her house.

Despite my deceit, I felt that I had triumphed over my own desires. The cool exterior I had displayed belied the raging fire that was tormenting me inside. All through dinner my desire had grown, I'd be faced with the sight of the tight white t-shirt, and I can't deny that there hadn't been hope of something physical later in the evening, but I wasn't going to rush things.

Okay, so she hadn't invited me in for coffee, but I didn't try to persuade her otherwise. I had respected her wishes. I had kissed her on the cheek, and not slobbered all over her.

If she thought I had treated her with respect and as an equal human being then that was perfect, because that's exactly what I had done. Of course there was an ulterior motive to my actions, there always is with men. I'd would love to have a coffee with her, but I was prepared to take things slowly.

Hopefully there'd be other opportunities for coffee, but the night was now at an end. I went home, put the kettle on, and drank alone.

- SIX -

The next morning I realised that Bob Geldof and I agreed on one thing, we both disliked Mondays. The weekend was just a distant memory, and the next one a whole five days away. I'd had an awful night's sleep. I was playing the date over in my mind, trying to find the moment when I should have admitted my lies, but each time I got as far as the jumper coming off and I got distracted.

So, I was tired and my working day was frustrating I ran around and tried to get a few assigned pieces finished. The people who I needed to speak to were unavailable and, although I left messages, they were never returned.

When they needed someone to cover a story, big or small, newspaper and magazine editors contacted me. They also used me to write features to fill gaps. I was a fill-in when they'd run out of staff, but thankfully there was enough fallback for me to make a living. I like to call myself freelance, but I might as well be on the payroll of most of the publications that used my services.

I decided to stop by the office to see if there were any messages for me and I bumped into the editor who informed me that the piece I was working on for the following week's paper, was actually for this week's, and I needed to pull my finger out. He shouted and told me that there were plenty of freelances out there who would be glad of the work if I wasn't up to it.

Freelance doesn't mean that you are your own boss, it means that everyone else is.

"Coffee?" said the Receptionist.

"Yes please. Extra caffeine if you have it," I said.

"Coming right up sir.' She gave me a mock salute and headed

to the kitchen. She returned a few minutes later with a mug and handed it to me.

"Why do you let him shout at you like that?" she asked.

"He's worked hard to get his blood pressure that high, shouting at me helps him maintain that level."

"Have you got a lot to do?"

"Nothing that can't be finished if I don't put my whole life on hold for a few days."

"What plans can a recently dumped man have?"

"Wow, you really know how to irritate a raw wound don't you?"

"Well, have you got plans?"

I shrugged. "That's not the point, I'm having to put the plans I might not have, on hold to deal with a deadline I didn't know about. Actually, I'll have you know I had a date last night. Thanks for the recommendation by the way."

"I assumed it was for a family birthday."

"No, it was a date," I said smugly.

"You do know that your right hand doesn't class as a date, don't you?"

"It was with a woman, and before you ask I didn't pay for her services either."

"Really? That makes a change."

"Look, I've never paid for sex in my entire life."

"You were engaged, you've been paying for sex for ages. You just didn't know it." She slapped me on the shoulder. "Now get on with your work, boy." She walked away and left me with my impossible deadline.

It took most of the day, and I still hadn't managed to finish. The Receptionist's mention of being dumped had rekindled some old memories. I tried to blot them out with thoughts of my potential new relationship, but both subjects meant I struggled to think straight. I eventually gave up and headed out for some air.

When you've had a bad day, walking past a pub without going into it is a physical impossibility. So I sat alone in a deserted bar and nursed a half empty glass.

The barman had served me and returned to his bar stool to continue reading his newspaper. Somehow, despite the ban, the place managed to smell of stale cigarettes, although I hated the smell it was preferable to actual smoke.

I studied the condensation running down the glass and took stock of my present situation. I was currently sat in a bar when I should have been working, that wasn't the most promising start. The woman I was possibly dating thought I was a tree hugging, animal loving vegetarian, when in fact I was a carnivore with a penchant for chasing cats with a pressure washer, and an ardent supporter of by-passes, if they shaved a few seconds off my journey. I had done nothing to dispel this image.

I was still upset about being the jilted boyfriend, and now I had added a different sort of stress to my circumstances. I missed Tin-man. If she'd been around, I'd be able to finish my drink and go back to her. In fact I probably wouldn't have been sat there in the first place because she'd have wanted me home.

Was I that desperate for female company that I was prepared to lie? I was berating myself for getting into my current situation, and I shook my head at my own stupidity.

"Penny for them," the voice belonged to a barmaid who had sneaked behind the bar without me noticing.

"I could probably get more at an internet auction," I said.

"Yes, but you'd never get to meet the buyer."

I drained my glass. "In your case, that would be a shame."

She was slim and had shoulder length brown hair with blonde streaks, or blonde hair with brown streaks, it was difficult to tell. Her full cheeks immediately made me think of a hamster. I was drawn to her. She was pretty, not gorgeous, but she had the ability to draw my attention completely.

"Let me fill that for you." She took the empty glass from my hand.

As she walked to the beer tap, I studied her a little more closely. I couldn't quite put my finger on it, but there was something about her that I found alluring. I was still staring when she came back and put the beer down in front of me. I reached into my pocket for some money, but she put her hand on my other arm.

"Have that one on me, you look like you need it." She winked a hazel eye. The lashes were so long that I could swear I almost felt the breeze that the movement caused.

She held out her hand and introduced herself. I shook it gently and returned the introduction. She settled herself on a stool the other side of the bar and said, "Want to talk about it?"

Ah, it all became clear. The age-old myth that bar-staff were the poor man's psychologists was true. I'd pour out my soul, she'd pour the drinks. I guessed that the free drink was a loss-leader. At some stage later in the day I'd stagger out of the bar, heavy in drink and lighter in the wallet.

Whatever hold she had over me was too strong. I told her about the stresses of work, the issue with my previous relationship, and the events that had led me to being sat in the bar with no desire to go home to an empty house. I told her everything... well almost everything. I left out the bit about Right-on. After all she was showing an interest in me and I didn't want to disappoint her.

A few more customers arrived. Her colleague remained seated at the opposite end of the bar still reading his newspaper, so she served the newcomers. She met each one with a smile and pleasant conversation. She had the same mesmerising effect on everyone, especially the men. When she had served each person, she retuned to the bar stool and we continued our counselling session.

I was acutely aware that I looked like one of those men with a girlfriend working in a bar, a man so insecure about his relationship that he had to be with her every minute of her working day. This sort of behaviour is peculiar only to the partners of bar staff. I have never yet been to the bank and found the teller's jealous boyfriend sat on a stool, watching her count money and cash cheques. Barmaids simply attract insecure men.

Her personality didn't just bubble, it fizzed. She gave me her complete and undivided attention, making me feel as though I was the only person in her world. Although I did most of the talking, I learned that she studied tourism at college, and the bar job was only part time. She lived alone in a small rented flat, and she was single.

She boosted my ego and made me feel good about myself. Despite my passionate hatred of cigarettes, I didn't even mind when she made her excuses and popped outside for a 'break', returning a few minutes later smelling of fresh smoke.

Whenever you're lured into the the trap of guessing a woman's age, always make the most conservative estimate that you possibly can…and then subtract three years. Unless you're incredibly unlucky you'll be way below the mark, and she'll be flattered. I'd guessed she was 20 when if fact she was 22.

She'd said I was 26 and I faked amazement, and told her she was exactly right. Yes, I stupidly knocked 10 years off my age. I was enjoying her conversation and lied for the same reason I hadn't mentioned Right-on.

Our chat was punctuated by her either serving customers or running off for an unscheduled lung cancer break. It had become dark outside and I looked at my watch. Bloody Hell! I'd been in the same place for three hours. I should have been home ages ago, tucked up in bed, so I could be fully prepared for the next morning.

While she was distracted with other customers, I readied myself to leave and stood up, or at least I thought I had. Although the message left the brain, it never quite reached the legs and I remained seated. A few moments elapsed and I suddenly appeared to be taller. I looked down and saw that the legs had finally responded. I was standing. I don't know whose legs I was using, but I was standing.

"Are you going?" Hamster Chick asked, when she returned from her serving duties.

Not on these legs I thought, and quickly sat back down. I have no idea how much I'd had to drink but it was obviously too much, this wasn't going to end well. "You'd better fill that glass up again," I said.

Sometime later, the newspaper addicted barman stood up and rang the bell for last orders. Satisfied that he'd done his work for the evening, he sat back down and resumed his reading. I don't remember him do anything else all night, surely one paper couldn't sustain a man for all that time. I wrote the stuff that filled some of those things, and I never found them that interesting.

I didn't want to look like I was drunk. I concentrated hard on not slurring my words, I made my movements slow and deliberate. All the signs that indicate someone is drunk.

"I'd better be going," I said.

Hamster Chick looked disappointed. "How about we make a night of it?"

A night of it? How much more of the night could there be left? "I really ought to leave."

"Why break up a beautiful friendship? C'mon I could probably find a good party."

My body refused, but some weak part of the mind crumbled. She grabbed a small handbag from beneath the bar and headed for the door, calling for me to follow. I went after her, I couldn't resist, I was hooked. I diverted all my resources to ensure that I walked in a straight line, but I know I bounced of some furniture and a couple of other drinkers, like a wayward pinball. Once outside, she expertly lit a cigarette, grabbed my hand and led me away from the pub.

Within a few minutes I found myself stood outside a fast food takeaway with the largest doner kebab I could carry. As I drunkenly munched my way through it, I realised that it was the first meat I had eaten in almost two days. It was greasy, unidentifiable goodness. Next to me, still dressed in her work clothes of black trousers and white shirt, Hamster Chick nibbled away at a smaller version.

It was good to have female company. Okay, so she thought I was ten years younger than I actually was, but unless she managed to get her hands on a copy of my birth certificate, it wasn't a problem. There was the added bonus that she'd paid for the kebab.

Two bus rides and a short walk later, I was standing outside a large factory on a disused industrial estate, in the middle of nowhere. The journey sobered me up slightly and I was pleased to discover that the pounding sound shaking my head was not the onset of an early hangover, but some late night construction work being carried out inside the factory.

Hamster Chick spoke to an overweight, denim-clad man stood outside the door. His hair was grey and unkempt, and he had a couple of days beard growth on his face. He looked me up and down and raised his bushy eyebrows. He made some disparaging comment to Hamster Chick about my clothes.

The cheek! I may well be drunk, but at least I was wearing a smart pair of trousers, a shirt, and tie. What did some failed rock band roadie know about fashion?

Hamster Chick spoke to him, his harsh expression melted into a hypnotised stare. How did she do that? He jerked his head in the direction of the open doorway and she pulled me through it.

The moment we entered the building, my ears were assaulted by a beat that sounded like a cannon going off. Somewhere behind it, other instruments struggled to be noticed. So it wasn't construction work, it was music, it was just someone needed to turn the bass down a bit. The whole place was filled with people jumping up and down whilst they waved their arms in the air. It was if someone had drained all the water out of a swimming pool full of drowning people.

The ghosts of the long departed machinery had left behind the heavy scent of industrial oil, tainted with a hint of damp.

It was dark, specks of light bounced off a disco glitter ball, spinning somewhere in the neglected rafters. Dancers spun torches and waved the type of glow sticks usually used by fishermen.

"C'mon," Hamster Chick shouted into my ear, "let's dance."

She took my hand and dived into the bouncing throng of

bodies. I dodged and swerved behind her and narrowly avoided getting swiped by erratic hand movements. She stopped right in the middle of the crowd.

I can't dance, I don't have the rhythm gene. Hamster chick raised both arms in the air. She moved her head from side to side whilst jerking her body in time to the beat.

Unlike a nightclub there was no free space to stand and watch the dancers; the whole building was a dance floor. I tried to bounce in time to the music, because it seemed to be the thing to do. I watched the other people and picked up a new move here and there. In no time at all I was a fully-fledged raver.

Whenever I went to a night club I was always self conscious. I thought that others were stood on the side-lines watching me and critiquing my dancing style, or rather lack of it. Because that's what I did.

I found this 'let-yourself-go-crazy' style of dancing strangely liberating, although the amount of alcohol in my system probably helped. I knew I wasn't being watched because there was nowhere to stand and do it, and my fellow ravers seemed to be lost in their own little world, eyes tight shut as they jumped for all their worth.

We didn't speak, we couldn't, it was too noisy, we just danced and smiled at each other. Hamster Chick had unbuttoned her shirt and, whenever she bounced I caught a glimpse of the lacy bra that restrained her ample breasts. She loosened my tie, and undid the top two buttons of my shirt that was now wet with sweat.

To my untrained ear, all the songs sounded similar and there was no break between them. There was no natural pause, or even a slowing down that meant I could stop. It was one continuous rhythm, I couldn't distinguish where one ended and another started. If it had been more obvious, I'd have had some idea of how long I'd been dancing. All I knew was that I was out of breath. My head was still fogged with the alcohol and I needed a drink, preferably not beer.

As if she'd read my mind, Hamster Chick leaned forward and

cupped her hand round my ear. "Let's get some air," she shouted, then turned and weaved her way through the crowd. I followed her as she went through a side door and out into the cool night. My wet shirt instantly became icy cold and stuck itself to my body. My ears rang, and despite being outside, the drumbeat was still shaking my bones as well as what was left of the factory windows.

The sudden change of temperature hit me like a train. My legs were like jelly and my breathing was laboured. I was feeling every one of my 26 years.

"Forgotten all your problems now?" She continued to dance and her body still twitched in time to the vibrating windows.

I nodded.

"A few minutes of fresh air and we'll go back in." She lit up a cigarette, took a huge draw and exhaled quickly, blowing the smoke into my face. Before I had chance to cough, she threw her arms around my neck and kissed me hard on the lips. She took me completely by surprise and I didn't respond straight away.

It was an intense, full-on kiss where she tried to get as much of her tongue into my mouth as possible. As good as it felt, I was acutely aware of a taste somewhere between an ashtray and kebab meat.

Out the corner of my eye, I caught the glowing end of a cigarette inches from my ear. The situation was precarious, I had no idea whether my hair gel was flammable or not. Any minute I could burst into flames. I'd run around like a human torch, screaming. Most people would think I was some sort of floor show. I wondered whether the factory was completely empty, or if there was still the odd fire extinguisher laying around. Having seen discarded bits of machinery, and random oil patches on the floor, I wasn't sure that the organisers were big on health and safety. It was then that I realised that I'd become detached from the situation. I concentrated on the kissing and I tried to push her tongue back into its own mouth.

I'd forgotten what it felt like to have someone else's lips touch mine. The last time I'd been kissed properly was by the

Tin-Man, and I tried to remember how it had felt, but I couldn't. It was probably because of the drink or the fact that my lips were currently pre-occupied with being attacked by an unknown mouth.

My thoughts were interrupted when she bit my bottom lip gently and then pulled away. When she let go it made a *'pup'* noise as it sprang back into place.

"Come on then, back inside."

"Where do you get all this energy from?" I asked.

"You really want to know?"

She put her hand inside her trouser pocket and pulled out a small resealable bag which contained three small white tablets. I'm not a pharmacist, but even I could tell that they were not painkillers. They weren't in a pop-out packet for a start.

I expected her stamina to be as a result of frequent visits to the gym, or some sort of freakishly large lung capacity. I hadn't entertained the idea that it might be chemically enhanced.

She emptied two of the tablets into the palm of her hand and held it out to me.

Apart from alcohol, nothing stronger than a paracetamol had ever entered my blood stream.

I looked at the tablets in her hand. This could be the start of the slippery road to addiction. An unfulfilled life lived from one fix to the next. Where a habit, funded by petty crime would eventually lead to me being found in a squalid bed-sit, covered in my own faeces, surrounded by needles having died of a heroin overdose. I realised that what little knowledge I had of drugs came from watching 'Train-spotting'.

I couldn't imagine that the manufacturer of these pills was particularly bothered with quality control, and I had heard of instances where tablets had consisted of Viagra and horse tranquillisers. If I was going to have an all night erection, I at least wanted to stay awake to reap the benefits.

The trepidation must have shown in my face. She thrust her hand forward. "You've done this before right?"

"Yes of course, loads of times." I used my thumb and forefinger to pinch one of the pills from her hand. I had bowed to peer group pressure, and there was only one other person in the group.

She slapped her open palm against her mouth, with her other hand she reached out and snatched a plastic water bottle from a passerby. When he protested, she flashed him that smile and he stopped dead in his tracks, then carried on walking, resigned to the fact he'd lost his drink. She took a sip from the bottle and threw her head back. She pushed the bottle towards me.

I was 36 pretending to be 26, at an illegal rave, and popping pills. My life had gotten strange in a short space of time. I examined the pill, there was the logo of a company roughly stamped onto it. Until that point I thought they'd only manufactured cars.

I dropped the pill on my tongue, grabbed the bottle from her and took a long swig. I was on my third gulp when my throat burned and my stomach contents tried to leave the same way they had gone in. What I had assumed was water, was in fact vodka. I had washed down my illegal substance with about a dozen shots of Russia's finest export. I coughed and spluttered, and I managed to turn my head away from Hamster Chick so that I did not spit second hand vodka all over her.

She laughed and patted me on the back.

"Wrong hole," I wheezed, as I pointed to my throat.

Hamster Chick grabbed my hand and pulled me in the direction of the entrance door, but I didn't move. My diminishing alcohol level had been given a boost. Going back inside would be disastrous. The jumping and the heat would be too much. I had that excessive drunken feeling that told me that a single false move would have resulted in a vomit situation.

She pulled me with both hands and I moved forwards. I concentrated really hard on my breathing. The sick moment passed, but I still needed to stall for time. I pulled her back towards me, wrapped my arms around her and kissed her.

I was completely committed to my action and I had no idea how long I could keep it going. There was no taste of cigarettes this time, but that was probably something to do with the flavour of vodka and bile in my own mouth.

She suddenly pulled away from me and squealed, "Oh, come on I love this song."

Even sober, I would not have been able to separate it from the previous one. She turned and headed for the door. I had no choice but to follow. She had been the only thing holding me up, and now she was gone, there was every chance I would end up on my ass.

She opened the door and dived straight back into the crowd. She'd let go of my hand so I was a little way behind, and I lost sight of her for a few seconds. When she reappeared she was jumping up and down and beckoning for me to join her.

I took one step towards her, it suddenly went dark and the music stopped. I fell forward, convinced I had blacked out, but I could still hear the sounds of screams and feet as they thundered around me. As I headed for the floor, the message from the brain to the arms, to tell them to brace themselves for impact, never got there and I fell face down. My chin's impact with the hard floor triggered a flash of white light. I had a grandstand view as hundreds of feet ran in all directions. The world started to spin and made me feel queasy again. My body became extremely heavy and I welcomed the rest. The combination of drink, pain in my chin, and probably that pill, made me want to sleep.

I lay there as the high-pitched screams gradually subsided and the footfalls became slower. My cheek was against the concrete floor. I was grateful for its coolness, I could relax and give in to the tiredness. Finally I submitted to sleep.

"Come on, wake up," I heard someone say.

Gravity weighed heavily on my whole body and any form of movement was impossible. I couldn't lift my head. I strained my eyes to try to look up, but it was pointless.

Someone grabbed hold of the collar of my shirt and lifted the top half of my body off the floor a few inches.

The stern voice spoke again and shook me as it did. "Come

on, on your feet."

However much I tried to lift my head, it sagged forward attracted to the floor like a magnet. I only succeeded in turning it slightly and I saw a pair of shiny, black shoes…and I threw up on them.

- SEVEN -

The dull throbbing in my chin combined with the same feeling in my head, and woke me up. I couldn't open my eyes straight away. I lay there and tried to regain full consciousness. A solid lump of unplanned wood filled my mouth, when it moved I realised it was my tongue. I remembered going to a bar, travelling on a bus, and having been to a rave. Oh, and of course there was Hamster Chick.

How long had I been out? I lifted my right wrist towards my face. I squinted and blocked out as much of the harsh artificial light as possible, whilst I looked at my watch. I had difficulty focussing and it was a few seconds before I realised my wrist was bare. Instinctively I lifted my body to feel my back pocket. My wallet was missing too. Bastard! I'd been robbed.

In an ill thought out action, I slapped my hand to my forehead in dismay, and let out a yelp as it sent a jolt of pain that shook my brain. Bastard, bastard, bastard! I pushed myself up on one arm. I definitely wasn't in the factory, it was too bright. I was in a room that was about twelve feet square and painted entirely in glossy magnolia. Underneath me was an inch thick, plastic covered mattress. There was a single door but no windows. It wasn't the factory, it wasn't my own room and, unless she was a minimalist, it definitely wasn't Hamster Chick's flat.

I sat up and shouted tentatively, "Hello?"

There was no reply.

I shouted a little louder, but still no one replied.

I stood up and stepped towards the door. I didn't even manage two steps, when my trousers slipped down to my ankles and I stumbled forward; I was no longer wearing my belt. As I bent down and pulled up my trousers, I noticed my shoe laces were also missing. Oh come on! What sort of sicko takes your watch, wallet, belt, and laces?

I held the waistband of my trousers and with the other I grabbed for the door handle, but there wasn't one. The smoothly painted surface of the glossy, blue door had only one feature; a tennis ball sized window at eye level. I put my hand on the door where there should have been a handle. It was just flat, cold metal. Panic set in and I banged on the metal door with my fist.

'Shut it!', a deep male voice boomed.

That was it, I'd been kidnapped by a madman, intent on killing me, or worse. I had no desire to be used as a sex toy by a psychopath. I tried not to think about what sort of degradation I'd been subjected to whilst I was unconscious.

I stood and checked whether I had pain anywhere. No, I was ok. Only my head and my jaw hurt so I hadn't been violated. Mind you my jaw hurt, what if he'd…Oh God no!

I had no idea what to do. I paced up and down, which was difficult considering I had no shoe laces and had to hold onto my trousers. I decided against screaming and shouting, in case it enraged my captor or even worse, excited him. If I remained quiet would he see this as a sign of weakness and think I was submissive? I decided to sit tight and keep my mouth shut.

I sat on the plastic mattress and hugged my knees to my chest. Without my watch I had no idea how long I'd been motionless, before I heard voices just outside the door. I went to the little window and peered out cautiously. The glass was cloudy, and smeared with something unspeakable. I tried to get a look at my captor.

There were two of them stood so close to the door that I could only see their heads. I had never seen anyone who looked more like a sadistic serial killer than the first man, well except for the man stood next to him.

The first one had a drawn face, under-lined by a closely trimmed beard. He had wide staring eyes. The second was much larger with a shaven head, and a very thin moustache. I was sure

I had seen their faces on 'Crimewatch'. They had, 'predatory, sexual deviant', stamped all over them.

Two men; that explained how they had transported me. One of them would hold me down whilst the other performed all sorts of sexual acts. When they'd finished, I'd be murdered and buried in a shallow grave. I'd be reported missing and, as I'm sure my parents didn't own a photo of me beyond the age of seven, they'd have to use the one from my passport which made me look like the serial killer. I'd probably never be found and I'd eventually be forgotten. In years to come I'd be the subject of one of those documentaries about missing people that appear on obscure television channels.

I couldn't let that happen. I wanted to keep my dignity, and more importantly, all my orifices intact! I wouldn't go down without a fight and, if they made me go down, I'd keep my mouth tightly shut.

A wide eye appeared in the window. "This one's ready," a voice shouted.

Damn right I was ready! I stepped away from the door. I clenched my fists by my side and readied myself. I could take these guys. I'd watched a couple of 'Bruce Lee' films when I was younger. I was going to have to fight for my life, I was prepared to battle to my very last breath, I hoped they were too.

My heart pumped, the adrenalin rushed around my body. My breath and pulse quickened. The key slid into the lock and turned. There was a click and the door opened. My two captors stood in the door way.

I immediately dropped to my knees. My head sunk to my chest. I clasped my hands together, and pleaded, "Please don't rape me."

The two men towered over me menacingly, and burst into laughter. I looked up, my captors were wearing police uniforms.

"You flatter yourself sweetheart, you're not that good look-ing,' said the thinner one. He stood in the doorway and mo-tioned for me to stand up.

I moved towards the open doorway. One captor walked

away and nodded his head in the direction he was moving. "Come on, follow me."

Suddenly it dawned on me. The locked room with no handle, my missing property, the men in police uniform; I had been arrested.

"Oh, thank God for that," I said, "you're police officers."

"Yes, we are and I don't know what cells you've been in before, but here we don't tend to bugger our prisoners."

"No, sorry. That was a misunderstanding," I said.

"I should hope so, I prefer my dates to be covered in a little less vomit." He winked at me.

I forced a laugh and followed one of the officers while the other fell in behind me. I walked along the corridor, and as I passed a closed door, the occupant banged on it hard and I jumped.

"You, you little bastard, you kept us up all night with your screaming and shouting," an angry voice yelled.

My lace-less shoes slopped like flip flops as I shuffled away from the door as quick as I could.

"Have I been noisy?" I asked.

"Oh yes, proper little banshee you were. That's why we put you all the way down here, so we didn't have to listen to you."

"How long have I been here?" I said to the cop in front.

"Oh, almost ten hours," he said.

"Ten hours!" I spat the words out.

"Yep, we were almost about to start charging you rent."

"What did I do? Why am I here?"

"The sergeant will explain everything."

Sandwiched between the two cops, I was led through a maze of corridors that continued the magnolia colour scheme from my cell. We eventually arrived at a large room. At one end was a counter, the surface was at chest height. Behind it, sat in an elevated position, was another uniformed officer.

I was escorted to the counter by my captors and left to stand directly in front of it, like a naughty child visiting the headmaster. The officer looked at me. He craned his neck forward and looked over the small round lenses of the glasses, that were perched on the end of his nose.

"Name?" he said sternly.

"Sorry sir, I'm not sure what's happening."

"It's not sir, it's sergeant. Now what's your name?"

I gave the sergeant my name and any other details he asked for. Eventually, he explained that I had been arrested after I had thrown up on a police officer's shoes.

"I am so sorry," I said, "it was the drink and the…" I was about to say "drugs" but stopped myself just in time. I didn't want to give the police an excuse to pull on a pair of rubber gloves, slap on some lubricant, and start exploring places that only a proctologist should go.

The sergeant explained that I had been arrested for being drunk and disorderly and, if I admitted my wrong doing, I would be released with a fixed penalty ticket.

"I only threw up, it that classed as being drunk and disorderly?" It was a genuine question, but I think it came across as belligerent.

The sergeant pushed his glasses up to the bridge of his nose, folded his arms and leaned them on the desk.

"Were you drunk?" he asked.

"Well…yes," I said.

"And would you say that puking on a police officer's shoes is orderly behaviour?"

"No, I don't suppose it is."

"Well, if it's not orderly then, by definition it must be disorderly."

I couldn't argue with his logic.

He handed me a piece of paper which detailed a fine that I would have to pay.

"Does this make me a criminal?" I asked.

"No," he said, "but it's still early yet."

He produced an A4 sized bag, and emptied the contents onto the counter top. My credit and bank cards fell out, along with my wallet, and the condom, that had been waiting patiently since my date with Right-on. I was reunited with my belt and shoelaces. There was a brown envelope containing some loose change and an alien packet of cigarettes

"These aren't mine," I said holding up the box.

"They were on you when you came in, we have to give them back."

I turned the packet around and there was a phone number written on one side. It was underlined and followed by the words '*call me*'. There was a small cross after it. It was either a kiss, or Hamster Chick was illiterate and it was her signature.

"This officer will show you out," the sergeant said pointing to the thinner one of my sexual predators.

I scooped up all my items with the hand that wasn't holding onto my trousers, and shuffled after the officer. He opened a door into a very short hallway, with a second door at the other end. The predator locked the first door behind us before unlocking the second one. He pushed it open and I stepped through it.

"Alright then," he said, with an air of finality.

I turned, "Can you apologise to the officers from last night please?"

The door was already closing when I heard him say, "Will do."

I'd been ejected into the middle of a busy city street. I shoved my personal property into my pockets and then slid my belt through my trouser loops.

I retrieved my shoelaces from my pocket, with them came a handful of coins that scattered across the pavement. I knelt down to pick them up and the porridge that was my brain slopped to the front of my skull. It had been raining during the night and the knee of my trousers soaked up an uncomfortable amount of water.

Whilst still kneeling in the wet, I rethreaded my shoelaces, and noticed that passers-by were deliberately avoiding me. They had seen me released from police custody and, unsure of what heinous crime I had committed, wanted to steer clear.

Before everything had gone wrong the previous day, I had

planned to work. Earning money was even more important, since there was the matter of a fine to pay. I stood up and brushed myself down. The newspaper office wasn't too far away, but I couldn't visit. I was covered in dried vomit and I looked like I'd slept in my clothes, which is exactly what I'd done. I had the appearance and aroma of a wino.

I had to go home first.

- EIGHT -

Fresh from a shower, I laid down on my bed and took stock of my situation. Within one week I had pretended I was vegetarian, taken ten years off my own age, attended a rave, taken drugs, vomited on a policeman, and been arrested.

On the plus side, I had two potential girlfriends. I battled with my hangover and wondered how I was going to make a choice about which one to date.

I should've been up and working, but my thoughts and my lack of any quality rest, meant I dropped off to sleep.

I drifted into a dream. I was dancing at a rave. Lights flashed but there was no music. I was dancing with Right-on, she was wearing that thigh length sweater. She pulled it over her head and slid it off in what was the start of a strip tease. Her magnificent breasts were restrained by that tight white top. She grabbed the hem of that top and started to slide it over her head. It came off quickly to reveal a five foot tall chicken drumstick. I threw my arms around it and nibbled the thigh, the nibbling was suddenly reciprocated. I pulled away and stared at a big, burly policeman. I threw up and the copper grabbed me and bundled me into a nearby cell. I fell and turned round just in time to see him, arm-in-arm with Tin-man, and she was wearing a wedding dress. They were both pointing at me and laughing.

The sound of my phone ringing rescued me from what had become a nightmare. I fumbled for the handset and answered it.

"Where are you?" It was the voice of the Receptionist.

"Sorry, I've been a bit busy." I hoped my voice didn't betray the fact I'd been asleep.

"I've got some assignments and you've got a bundle of work that needs to be submitted. If you don't get it sorted our friend with the high blood pressure is going to find someone else."

"Ok, I'll be there shortly," I said.

"You'd better be, I'm not performing the kiss of life on the old git if his heart gives out."

As I readied myself to leave the house, I couldn't shake the image of Tinman in the wedding dress, that the dream had left etched on my mind.

I would have gladly swapped work for an afternoon on my own in front of the television, but I had learned a long time ago not to turn down any jobs, however minor they may seem, otherwise you get yourself a reputation for being awkward and the work just dries up. Money is money, however hard you have to work for it.

I dressed quickly and hurried to the office. I avoided the wrath of the editor with the high blood pressure and collected a handful of assignments from the Receptionist.

Running a long distance for nothing more than charity, strikes me as an astonishingly stupid thing, but I suppose there must be a feel good factor to it somewhere. That's exactly what the subjects of my first assignment were doing.

As arranged, I found the group of sporty-looking women in the middle of the park. As I got closer I began to wish I'd paid a little more attention to my own appearance. They had finished their training, and were all engaged in various exercises, which meant I got a good look at their physiques; their tight vests and shorts which revealed more of their bodies than they probably intended.

The sight of taut buttocks put me into a trance like state. I had just realised I looked like some sort of pervert, when a real pervert actually turned up in the form of Macro-Mike, the over-weight newspaper photographer. With questionable personal hygiene, and even more questionable morals, I had concerns about Macro; 'exposure' was clearly more to him than just a photographic term.

I snapped out of my trance as some of the women eyed me with suspicion. I started to talk, and the leader of the pack stepped forward, she looked ready to castrate me, but softened slightly when she saw the man with the camera, which is ironic considering the thoughts that would have been going through Macro's head. I introduced myself.

The short walk from the car park meant that Macro was breathing heavily and sweat had broken out on his greasy face. He placed his camera bag on the floor and fiddled with the lenses of the two cameras strapped around his neck, lenses that were quite obviously meant for peering into bedroom windows from long distances. As he pushed his subjects into lines and tried different poses, Macro's hands lingered long enough to be awkward. I could tell what he as thinking but thankfully, the women couldn't. If ever a camera needed an anti-shake, it was the one Macro held.

I became professional and asked all the right questions. The ladies were all from the same gym, and they were running in aid of a cancer charity, in memory of a friend who had died the year before.

I took the names of all the runners. Although a lot of newspapers are now online, it's a fact that people will still buy a newspaper if their name or photograph appears in it. People like to see themselves in print. I went along the line getting their names and ages. I hadn't really taken any notice of them, well not their faces anyway. Then there she was. A vision in a vest. Her slim figure evidence of hours spent in a gym. Her blonde hair was in a bob style which she kept tucking behind her ears whenever she spoke. It was too short to stay put, so she continually repeated the action. She either needed longer hair or bigger ears.

I was so busy studying her that I didn't hear any of the details she gave me, and I had to ask her again. This time I paid attention and tried to extend our meeting, but there are only so many questions you can ask someone who is going to run a marathon. What's your target time? How often do you train? Is it true you have to abstain from sex before a race? Maybe the last one was boxing.

It was over all too quickly, and they gathered their things and made their way home.

Macro and I walked away and he made a few comments that, had he worked in an office, would have earned him a written warning, but man to man I guess he figured he'd be safe. I joined in and made a couple of awkward, lame jokes. I'm a red-blooded male, in certain circles it's expected, if not encouraged.

It started to rain and as I hurried back to my car I caught sight of the attractive marathon runner. She was running towards the exit of the park and, in an effort to protect her from the rain she held a small sports bag above her head. I watched her for a while, until it became apparent that she wasn't heading to a car.

I drove out of the car park and pulled the car alongside her. At first she didn't stop, in fact she moved faster. I opened the passenger window.

"Can I give you a lift?" I shouted.

She bent down and looked inside, probably checking for any weapons, or a bottle of chloroform. She was understandably very cautious. She glanced around as though she was checking to see if anyone was looking, and I was struck by the fact that if anyone was watching, then they would have probably mistaken me for a kerb crawler.

I was convinced that she was about to refuse when the heavens opened and there was a sudden, even heavier, downpour.

When she had decided I probably wasn't a risk, she pulled open the door, climbed in and sat down. She clicked the seatbelt into place and then wiped her hair away from her face. This time, because it was wet, it stayed in place behind her ear.

"You're very kind," she said.

"I'm a sucker for a damsel in distress."

"As someone who is going to run a marathon, I really should be walking."

"Not in this weather you shouldn't. You should be in a nice

warm gym," I said.

"That would be preferable. Do you go to the gym?" she asked.

Considering my track record with regards to lying, I know what you're thinking, but it would have been blatantly obvious from my expanding mid-rift, that I had been nowhere near a gym in quite some time. In fact it had been several years since I had done anything that could be faintly misconstrued as exercise. No, I wasn't about to make up some desperate lie again, especially one that could be so easily disproved.

If I didn't eat meat I could pretend I was a vegetarian. Due to my liberal use of after-shave moisturiser, I could just about fake being ten years younger, but I would never be able to hide the fact that walking up a flight of stairs made me out of breath. No, I would be honest with this woman. There was no room in my life for more deceit.

"I'm not really a regular visitor to the gym," I said patting my stomach. "I used to be quite active, but to be honest I think I've let myself go a bit."

"No, I think you look g..." She stopped short and I saw her blush.

Well, what was it, "Good"? "Gross"? "Gargantuan"?

We chatted as she directed me to the home she shared with her parents. As I pulled to a stop outside a detached house with a wide gravel driveway, she un-clicked her seatbelt and then touched my hand which was still on the gear stick.

"Thank you again."

She stepped out of the car and closed the door. Before I knew what I was doing I lowered the window and called after her, "Do you fancy a drink sometime?"

She smiled and I wondered for a moment whether I'd overstepped the mark. She opened her sports bag and took out a pen. She scribbled on a piece of paper, folded it in half and then handed it to me. "Call me," she said.

"I will, bye."

"Goodbye, God bless," and with that she turned and walked towards the house.

I left it a couple of days before I called her, because I wasn't really sure why I'd asked another woman out on a date. I tried to justify it to myself. I had been on two dates with two different women. They weren't relationships as such, they were friendships with potential, and all I was doing was increasing my chances of success. I hadn't betrayed anyone. Besides lots of people played the field, why should I miss out? I had led a clean life, maybe I deserved a bit of fun.

No, I couldn't even justify my actions to myself.

So I made the phone call and she invited me for Sunday dinner.

- NINE -

There was an extra swagger in my step when I walked back into the newspaper office. Somehow I had become irresistible to women, it was a strange sensation and I wasn't altogether comfortable with it. Although it felt good, it was tinged with an inescapable guilt, a bit like winning the lottery with a ticket you'd found on the floor outside an orphanage. I'd happily reap the benefits, but there was no way I was confessing.

It was deadline day; people shouted, telephones rang, computer keyboards clattered. The editor with the high blood pressure tore a strip off his cub reporter for not putting three sugars in his coffee. The advertising sales reps in the next office, made frantic, last minute phone calls trying to sell vital column inches

I sat down at an empty desk and turned on the computer. As I waited for it to come to life, I allowed myself a smile. Ok, so it was more complicated than it had been several hours before, but my life had changed and with a little bit of common sense I thought I could juggle three women.

Suddenly my mobile phone rang. I looked at the display, it was Right-on. There was a pang of guilt caused by my deceit and the sudden realisation that I had not called her as promised. I hesitated for a second and wondered whether I should ignore the call and forget about her, but any uncertainty was overcome by the thought that, somewhere down the line, this phone call might eventually lead to a sexual experience, which involved more than just me.

I pressed the answer button. "Hi."

"Hi," she said. "Just checking you were okay. I've not heard from you."

"Sorry about that, jobs keep coming in thick and fast and I'm not really in a position to turn them down. In fact I'm at work at the moment." I hoped that she could hear the background chatter and the tappity-tap of the keyboards around me. I clicked the mouse and hammered a few random keys just to make sure. I didn't want her to think I was lying. Why it mattered that she did not suspect me of lying about the fact I was at work is a little confusing, considering that I had misled her about being a vegetarian.

"You've been busy then?" she asked.

I held the phone against my ear with my shoulder and continued typing. *Well, I chatted up another woman, ended up at an illegal rave, took some drugs, and then puked all over a policeman, which resulted in my arrest, and subsequent fine for being drunk and disorderly. Oh, and I've also arranged a date with yet another woman.*

"Yes, very," I replied.

"So are we meeting up again?"

"Yes, of course, just name the day and I'll be there."

"Are you sure you won't be busy?" she said.

"No, no I promise not to make other arrangements."

"That's good. Sunday then, 3 o'clock my place. I'll cook you dinner."

"Sounds great, I'm looking forward to it." And I meant it, I really was. Hopefully she did not wear that damn jumper in her own home.

"See you then, and don't be late."

"I won't. Bye."

"Bye," she said. I watched the phone's display until she had hung up. I clenched my fist and in a show of masculine bravado I shook my hand almost imperceptibly, and through clenched teeth I hissed, "Yes."

"Yes what?" said a voice.

I peered over the top of my computer monitor and looked at the quizzical face of the Receptionist.

"Nothing," I continued typing.

"Oh come on," she said, "you make a show of celebration and

it's for nothing. I don't think so." She raised her eyebrows. "Is it to do with your date from the other day? So tell all."

So I told her all about the three women in my life, my underhanded lying, and I even mentioned my arrest. I brought her right up to date with the phone call that had finished a few moments before.

I waited for the judgement, but what I got was a sigh and a shake of the head. "Wow, you really couldn't make that up," she said.

"No, that's one thing I haven't made up these last few weeks."

"So what are you going to do?"

"I don't know. I've had a really bad time recently and I need something good to happen in my life. Is it wrong to carry on seeing three different people, even if you haven't committed to them?" I was asking an honest question, to which I didn't know the answer.

"I suppose it depends on your definition of 'committed'. Put yourself in their position, if you were one of those three, don't you think you'd feel a bit betrayed?"

"Probably, but it's not like I can call any of them my girlfriend yet. I just want to see what happens."

"Ok, keeping your options open, I can understand that," she said, "but you still haven't told me what you intend to do?"

"I'll just have to wait and see which one turns into a relationship."

"By 'relationship' you mean which one sleeps with you first?"

I lowered my face behind the computer screen, and out of her sight to hide the blush that was creeping up my face.

"I've been struggling recently, three women have been a distraction from the pain of my break up. My confidence needs a boost. It's not always about sex you know."

"You keep telling yourself that if it makes you feel better," she said, "but that wasn't what I meant though, what are you doing this Sunday?"

"I'm sorry, I already have plans."

She laughed. "You flatter yourself, I don't fancy being part of your harem."

"What do you mean then?" I said.

"This is the problem you're going to have if you continue with your pretence."

I shook my head again. "I really don't understand what you're saying."

"There are two problems as I see it. You're telling lies to different people, it's going to be very difficult to keep track of what you've said, and to whom. And you're also going to have to get yourself a secretary, or at the very least a diary." She paused, and waited for this to sink in, it didn't. "You've got two dates on Sunday, Romeo."

My hands froze and my fingers hovered over the keyboard. The realisation dawned on me. I had made a right royal screw up. The Receptionist was right, I'd arranged two dates for Sunday.

"Oh God!" I rubbed my forehead with one hand. "This is a nightmare."

"Not really," the Receptionist said, "you'll just have to cut your dinner time date short so that you can get to your second date. It's all a case of time management."

"That's the least of my problems. I'm having tea with my parents on Sunday."

This triggered laughter.

"It isn't funny. What the hell am I going to do?"

"You'll have to cancel one of them," she said through snatched breaths.

"I can't."

"Why not?"

She was right, I could just call and cancel one of them, but which one? It was a long time since a woman had shown any interest in me. Cancelling was a rejection, and I'm not sure they'd stick around if I pulled out of our date. Like the Receptionist had said, I wanted to keep my options open.

"I like them both," I said.

"Well, as least cancel the dinner with your mother."

"Absolutely no chance! She'll have been preparing all week and she'll start cooking on Saturday night. She'll even make my Dad have a bath Sunday morning. Cancelling that is not an option."

"How about taking the Vulcan woman to you parents? That should kill two birds with one stone."

"It's vegan, not Vulcan,"

"What's the difference?"

"Someone who boycotts animal products is a vegan. Mr. Spock from 'Star Trek' is a Vulcan, and I'd rather take him to dinner with my parents on Sunday, it'd be easier to explain why my dinner companion is a fictional alien.

"I can't introduce her to my family just yet, any chance of a relationship will be destroyed the moment she walks through the door, and finds my Dad stood at the dining room table, sharpening a knife, ready to hack into half a cow."

There was no way I could take Right-on. Okay, I could contact my Mum first and tell her I had become a vegetarian, but that meant that my Dad would refer to me as a 'girl' for the entire time I was there. If I just kept quiet, it would be a matter of seconds before I was 'outed' as a meat-eater and my deception uncovered.

There was also another reason I could not introduce a new girlfriend to my family. There were two other potential girlfriends waiting in the wings, and it was possible that I may need to introduce one of them at some stage. However much my Dad would pat me on the back and say, "Good lad", I could not bear to think of my mother's face as she looked at me with distaste when she realised that her only son was a man-whore.

"So, back to my original question. What are you going to do on Sunday?"

"I really don't know," I leaned back in the chair and looked at the ceiling, "maybe having three dinners won't be such a bad thing."

- TEN -

I gave a lot of thought to my predicament, although it was difficult, it wasn't impossible.

Historically, Mum always cooked Sunday dinner late in the day. If she remained true to form, the dinner table would be set for about 5pm. This meant that if I had dinner with the marathon runner at midday, I should be able to be with Right-On by 3pm. I could make my excuses and leave a little early, and get to the family meal by 5pm. As long as Hamster Chick didn't suddenly make an appearance and want a late lunch, it would work.

I was still sorting the logistics of the upcoming Sunday, when Bestie called and offered a distraction by way of a beer-soaked night, camping in the countryside.

So, just a couple of days before my big dates, I found myself bouncing around in the front seat of a car, as it travelled along a dirt track towards a campsite. The car jerked to a halt outside a garage type hut with the word, 'RECEPTION', stencilled on the surrounding brickwork.

I pushed open the door at the side of the sign and stepped inside, whilst Bestie went to find a pitch for the tent.

It was as though I'd stepped into a mirrored room, bisected by a long counter. The window and door on my side, were reflected on the opposite wall. The only thing that was missing from the image was another me. Brochures showing places of local interest were strewn across the counter.

I was flicking absent-mindedly through the leaflets when I found a black doorbell with a little white button. I pressed it and there was a distant, almost inaudible ring.

Through the window behind the counter I saw a large house on a small hill, a short distance away. It was old and in need of renovation; probably the home of the campsite owner. My thoughts kept being interrupted by irritating, scratchy snatches of violin music which, although I couldn't identify, was eerily familiar. No one had come out of the house as I had expected, and I was just about to reach for the button again, when the 'mirror' door opened and in walked Norman. Six foot two tall, stocky build, greasy black hair with grey highlights, and an expression that suggested his mother had just died.

There was no small talk or pleasantries. No, "Did you have a good journey?", "Have a nice stay", or "Would you like to see my taxidermy collection?". I paid for a pitch, and exchanged more money as a deposit for the key to the shower/toilet block, which was attached to a piece of wood that could also double as a coffee table.

The transaction over, Norman turned and left by the same door.

With the tent pitched, we met with one of Bestie's old work friends. We took two cars, parked one in a pub car park and then took the other about four miles down the road. The pub was the carrot to our donkey.

It wasn't a difficult walk. It was warm enough for t-shirt and shorts. We passed lush green meadows, ambled through shaded forests, and crossed gurgling streams. It was peaceful and I quite enjoyed myself.

It was only when we stumbled upon a small teashop called, 'The Rambler's Retreat', did mild panic set in. With absolutely no warning at all I had become a rambler. There had been no urge to pull my socks up on the outside of my trousers, or absent-minded buying of bobble hats, it had just suddenly happened. One minute I was normal, and then I was a rambler. I consoled myself with the thought that it was a one off. A walk to spend some time in a country pub away from female distractions.

The walk was long enough to make the pub a welcome sight. We stepped inside and a brace of locals stood at the bar. We were in the middle of nowhere. I took a back seat whilst Bestie and his friend explored old times. This was what I needed, to be listening to a conversation that didn't mention anything about me, women, weddings, or any other of the myriad of subjects that I could link to my predicament.

Life always has a way of pinching you back to reality. The first few notes of a song floated out across the bar and snatched away any feeling of contentment. It was 'our' song. All it needed was the sorrowful voice of Simon Bates and I could have had those locals sobbing into their real ale.

The voices telling tales of times gone by and past debauchery faded into the background. I excused myself, but the music was even being piped into the toilet. I supposed this was so participants in the Monday night pub quiz wouldn't miss anything, or maybe they hired the room out for parties. Literally unable to face the music, I stepped outside for 3 minutes and 14 seconds.

If you want my advice, and you're going to get it unless you skip the next two paragraphs, don't have an 'our song', it makes life too difficult. You have that special song that means so much and the moment you break up, you hear it everywhere. Radios, supermarkets, even lifts, will guarantee to stab you in the heart by playing it.

If you insist on having a song, make it something obscure that you're not going to hear anywhere other than in your own private record collection. An old friend of mine and his girlfriend, chose 'Last Christmas' as their song. Not a bad idea in the obscurity stakes, but unfortunately she left him for the postman. Now, for one month out of every twelve he can't listen to the radio.

The music and the memories assaulted my heart. I felt sad and realised that despite my recent escapades, I wasn't quite over the break-up. Was it what life was going to be like? Would I forever suffer from unexpected flashbacks? It was PTSD...Post Tinman Sadness Disorder.

I must have looked a little melancholy when I returned, but no one mentioned it. Bestie seemed to sense that something was not quite right and decided to drag me into the conversation.

As I sat down next to him, he gave me a nudge and said, "Tell him about your women."

"Women? Plural?" said ex-workmate.

"I've kind of found myself dating three women." I didn't want to go into all the details.

"How?'

"It just happened."

"Wow," he said, "for someone who's just been left at the altar, you don't let the grass grow under your feet."

Being jilted by my fiancee made me feel like I'd failed in some way, and I wasn't entirely comfortable with an complete stranger knowing about it. I silently thanked Bestie for sharing my recent failures, when he clapped me on the shoulder. "Never one to let a little set back like being dumped get him down. I'm so proud of him." He laughed and his friend joined in.

"Trust me, it's not all fun and games," I said.

"Three women?" said ex-workmate, "You're joking, it sounds great."

"It's not great, I only want one."

"I'll take one off your hands. I'll never turn down sloppy seconds."

I was repulsed by the image that had flashed into my mind, but let out a weak laugh. "Like I said, it's not as great as it sounds. I'm not entirely sure what to do."

"Well, can I offer you some advice that might help?"

I hadn't met this man before today, he was several years older than me, and I'd noticed he was wearing a wedding ring. I wasn't sure how helpful he could be in a situation he knew very little about, but perhaps the view of someone who was completely removed from the circumstances, and the participants was what I'd needed. Maybe someone who didn't know me, or the other parties involved would be the person who provided the perfect answer.

"Go on then," I said.

"Shag 'em, all three of them…at the same time." He roared with laughter. Bestie joined in and they clashed their pint glasses in a toast to their own masculinity.

And that's why men don't discuss their relationships issues with other men!

We fetched the car we'd abandoned at the beginning of our walk and took it back to the pub car park. Bestie's finest attempts at liquid exorcism meant that he had almost cleared the pub of spirits, so he decided it would be safer to leave his car there.

The rest of the night involved more alcohol and a stagger back to our canvas hotel.

My head was a fuzzy when I was woken by the voices of the occupants in the neighbouring tent. When I finally climbed out of the sleeping bag, I plodded off for a shower dragging the key attached to the coffee table behind me. From the outside the block looked like a large wooden hut, but when I opened the door I was pleasantly surprised at the, well I hasten to use the word, splendour. Neatly tiled, clean sinks, well scrubbed floors, and there were even hand towels. There was a linen basket for depositing the used towels, and there was music. Piping music into public conveniences must be a thing in this part of that country

The block was deserted and I headed for one of the shower cubicles accompanied by a soothing piece of music that, for a man suffering from the effects of a skinful of alcohol it was way too loud, and also for some reason left me slightly un-nerved. I stepped into the cubicle and suddenly remembered why I recognised this tune; it was the Goldberg Variations. I didn't know the name then, but I knew where I'd heard it last. It was the scene in the 'Silence of the Lambs' where Hannibal Lecter is in a cage waiting to be transferred somewhere, the scene that ends in bloody murder.

Thankfully, I didn't need to find coins for this shower, I was allowed as much hot water as I needed, but I showered quickly and as the words, "Ready when you are Sergeant Pembury," echoed inside my head, I left and went in search of somewhere to have breakfast. There had to be something to take the sting out of the hangover.

According to my camping and caravanning book the site had a restaurant, or at least that's what I thought that little crossed knife and fork icon meant, and I couldn't understand why we couldn't find it. I realised it wasn't a restaurant as Egon Ronay would have described it, in fact it wasn't even one that a certain fast food clown would have recognised. In fact it was another shed, a big one but nevertheless a shed.

I thumbed through my club book for the key. Aha! There it was, crossed cutlery means food! Food? What sort of description is that? An apple tree could be food. It was a, "coined phrase to encompass a broad spectrum of eating establishments", as Bestie eloquently put it. What did he know, he was hung-over!

Just to assure you at this point that when I refer to the site book as mine, it was simply in a present possessive kind of way. I had borrowed that book; I was in no way about to add 'caravanner' to the unwanted 'rambler' tag. A man can only attend so many support groups.

At one end of the shed stood a counter, with all the hallmarks of being rescued from a bankrupt butcher's shop. It was full of plastic wrapped sandwiches, pasties, and bottled drinks. Crammed into the shed was a wooden table that looked like it had been stolen from a beer garden. It had small benches on either side, just wide enough to accommodate an average sized bottom.. The irresistible smell of bacon and other fried foods knitted with the fibre of my clothes.

The 'Shed Café' also doubled as a shop and countless obscure items lined the shelves. Tinned kiwi fruit, an Ordnance Survey map of Bodmin Moor, a box of 110 film cartridges, and some brightly coloured children's fishing nets with long cane handles.

Previous patrons had probably made enquiries for items that weren't stocked, but the person behind the counter had logged the request and stocked up next time they went to the 'cash-and-carry', only for no one to ever ask for them again.

Two old ladies bustled about behind the counter. I checked to make sure one of them wasn't Norman. "Is there any chance of a bite to eat?" Bestie asked.

Without even turning around one woman answered in a strict schoolteacher voice, "It'll have to be quick, we close in ten minutes and I'm off to the Cash and Carry."

"Sit down," the other ordered.

Like her obedient schoolchildren, we sat at the table, one on either side to balance it out.

"I can only do you, sausage, egg, bacon, fried bread, mushroom, and black pudding," she said, and without even waiting for an answer she began cooking a '*quick*' breakfast.

She muttered to the other old dear, just loud enough so that we couldn't hear, but over-the-shoulder dirty glances suggested that their discussion was about our ignorance at having turned up just before the place was was due to close. I was uncomfortable and watched carefully in case anything I hadn't ordered went into my breakfast.

After a short while, a mug of tea landed unceremoniously in front of me with a clunk, some of its contents slopped onto the tabletop. It was swiftly followed by a plate which slid across from the end of the table, aqua-planed across the spilt tea, and nudged the mug enough to spill yet more liquid before it came to a stop.

As breakfasts go it looked impressive. I don't know whether it was the unwillingness with which it had been cooked, the off-handed flourish of the service, or the half pint of tea soaking into the fried bread, but I just didn't enjoy it.

The cook stood, arms folded, in the corner which because of the size of the shed wasn't that far away. Her presence suggested the need for us to hurry up, so we ate and drank quickly.

I put my knife and fork down and before they had finished clattering on the plate, everything was swiped away and dropped into a bowl somewhere behind me.

She stared at us until we got the hint. We stood up, paid the bill, and turned to leave. I stopped as I got to the doorway, "You haven't got any chargrilled tiger prawns in a hoisin sauce have you?"

Put that on your shopping list!

We'd been walking for what seemed like hours, but there was no sign of the pub we'd been in the night before. Perhaps it had been a dream. "Have you seen Brigadoon?" I asked. Bestie was grumpy. It was his car, why should I be the one to remember where he'd parked it?

For almost two hours I walked in silence, partly because we weren't talking but also the hangover thirst had gripped my throat and rendered speech painful, and almost impossible.

Up hill and down dale, through villages that would no doubt have been pretty, if it hadn't been for the banging headache and raging dehydration. The more I walked, the worse I felt. Each footstep resonated through my body, starting at the toes and finishing in the agonising mess that used to be my brain. I felt like a tuning fork. Nausea crept up from my stomach, and when I belched I could taste tea-soaked fried bread.

How can alcohol have such diverse affects? One moment you're giddy with happiness. You're confident enough to fight the local boxing champion, and convinced you're attractive enough to successfully chat up supermodels without fear of rejection. The next morning, you'd gladly cut off your own head with a penknife if it would get rid of the damn pain.

I vowed never to drink again; it was expensive and the drawbacks far outweighed the benefits. From this moment forward I would drink only at Christmas and birthdays, and then it would be moderately. I would never again fall foul of the evils of drink. I longed to be at home, curled up in bed, whimpering gently to myself.

My conversion to abstinence was interrupted by the appearance of our destination. We reached the brow of a the hill, and a shaft of sunlight lit up the small, thatched hostelry, in much the same way the star of Bethlehem lit up that stable. In fact I think I even heard a choir of angels.

With the last ounce of energy in my legs, I stumbled down the steep hill, my momentum quickly carrying me forwards. My arms flailed and my head lolled from side to side. There was a stupid grin on my face. I was lucky some local farmer didn't take me for a lunatic and shoot me.

When I finally reached my destination, I rested on a wooden gatepost. My head pounded with each heart beat and the return of breakfast was just one belch away.

Bestie looked at his watch, "Hair of the dog?"

- ELEVEN -

I wrote Friday off as a hangover recovery day, but I couldn't allow myself the luxury of a day off on Saturday. Usually when most people enjoyed the start of their weekends, I found myself working. My pending submissions for the newspaper, and a further two assignments for a magazine, meant that Saturday would be no different.

Since the start of my doomed engagement, I had been putting a bit of cash aside each week. Even though it was no longer needed, I'd avoided dipping into the wedding fund, just in case things should change. This suggested that I hadn't given up hope, part of me was still under the illusion that she would come running back, and everything would be as it was.

A few months previously I had been in, what I thought was a monogamous relationship, and I still felt the pain her bombshell phone call had caused when I'd received it; she couldn't even dump me face to face. It closed the gateway to my future and I found myself back on the shelf. Thankfully my place was still warm and the dust hadn't even had chance to settle. I admit I missed the comfort of that relationship.

How I had dealt with my situation? I had rebounded in stupendous style, straight into another woman, and then I'd ricocheted off into two others. Was I misleading them? Was it wrong to be involved in three relationships? There was no commitment to any of them. None of the relationships had been consummated. I wouldn't have described any of them as girlfriends. Until that point they had only been dates, nothing more. It was a bit like buying a car, you always went on a test-drive before you purchased. At the moment, all I was doing was admiring them through the showroom window.

If I'm honest, the whole thing was tainted with just a little bit of guilt. I couldn't be certain that what I was doing was right, but I was prepared to hang on just in case that feeling disappeared, or one of them gave in and had sex with me, whichever happened first.

Sunday; it was almost midday when I arrived at my first date. I had taken care over my appearance, but not to the same extent I had with Right-On. I hoped to God that the protein she needed to run that marathon came from meat, and not some vegetarian imitation.

Having showered and applied just a small spray of aftershave, I had chosen jeans and t-shirt. I didn't want it to look like I had tried too hard. I had placed the condom, that had accompanied me on my recent incarceration, into my pocket. I tried not to think of the possibility that there might be some sexual experience after dinner, but the fact I'd packed my little rubber friend suggested I was hopeful.

It's unusual to have a woman cook for you on your first date, so I wasn't sure whether this was a sign that she may want to take things further. Perhaps she was one of those women who wasn't bothered about the pre-amble that went with relationships and liked to become physical very quickly. I didn't know her at all and I had no idea what she had planned, but I wanted to be prepared for all eventualities.

In reality, considering my time constraints, it would be difficult to slip in a bout of intercourse before I left for my next date…even by my standards.

I stopped at the local supermarket, and bought a tasteful bunch of flowers, making sure to remove the 'reduced' stickers.

I knew she lived with her parents, but it struck me that I knew almost nothing about my date. I guess that getting to know someone is exactly what these events are for. An intimate home-cooked meal would be the ideal occasion. We could talk without me making a fool of myself in front of pretentious waiters. Yes, this would be perfect. The word, 'sex', momentarily peered around the thoughts of a civilised dinner and I tapped my pocket, checking I'd remembered the condom.

I crunched my way up the gravel drive, and pressed the door-bell. The door was opened by a middle-aged man in a shirt and tie, over which he had pulled a grey tank-top. He was almost bald, what little hair he had was plastered to his head with some sort of old man's hair product, which I could actually smell.

He looked me up and down, and took in my attempt at casual dress. There was an awkward few seconds where I thought I'd got the wrong address. I looked over my shoulder and back towards the road, I fully expected the man to throw the door open and shout, "Release the hounds!"

As I judged my chances of getting back to the car before being torn to shreds, my date appeared at the side of the man in the doorway.

"Hello," she said.

She had replaced the vest and shorts with a knee-length black skirt and a red blouse, making me feel a bit under dressed for the occasion.

"Come in," she said, "Dad, don't block the doorway."

So this was Dad, maybe "Release the hounds", was exactly what he was thinking.

I stammered a greeting and stepped over the threshold into the hallway. The warm smell of Sunday roast filled the air, destroying the aroma of whatever grease Dad was using on his scalp. I momentarily forgot my awkwardness, and thanked God that this was a meat-eating household. That thought was immediately replaced by the realisation that this was not going to be a cosy meal for two. If there was a Dad, then in all likelihood there'd be a Mum too. I'd jumped straight into a dinner with the parents of a woman with whom I'd only shared a short car journey. I was walking into the lion's den.

I was considering the speed with which this relationship had moved forward, when my date leaned over and kissed me on the cheek. Dad was watching me intently, so I denied myself the quick glance down the blouse that the opportunity presented, and accepted the greeting. I offered the flowers and her acceptance was accompanied by grateful cooing.

She officially introduced me to Father. There was a curt nod, accompanied by a handshake that was a little too strong and tight to be friendly. All the time his eyes drilled into me, I didn't let on that his grip hurt like hell. He made it clear that he was in charge. This one-way, world's strongest grip competition was only brought to a halt when the flowers were thrust towards Father, and he was asked to find a vase.

The pain had subsided and my hand almost regained its original shape, when it was grabbed again by my date. "Come and meet everyone else," she said as she pulled me along the hallway.

Before my mind could compute the words, "everyone else", she pushed open a door and dragged me into a sitting room. I say sitting room, but that would tend to suggest that there was actually somewhere to sit. There were chairs, but every one of them was taken.

Seven sets of eyes stared directly at me. I felt like the excommunicated family member at a funeral wake. I was introduced to each person and instantly forgot their names, and their place in the family tree. I remember a brother, possibly a cousin or two. An aged couple could only be a set of grandparents, from which side I didn't know.

I nodded and smiled.

"Is he the doctor?" said the old lady I assumed was someone's grandmother.

"No, Nan it's her new boyfriend," said someone who was possibly a brother.

"I'm not sure about boyfriend, well not yet anyway." My date smiled. She gave the hand she still held a gentle squeeze. Everything was happening way too quickly, and I couldn't help but feel just a little bit scared.

The door I had been ushered through opened again and in rushed a short woman wearing an apron. I didn't need to be a geneticist to work out that this was Mum. Although she had given her features to her daughter, some trace of their origins still remained in her face.

She dried her hands on a tea-towel as she spoke. "Ah, this is him is it? Pleased to meet you. The flowers are lovely," she said, offering a slightly damp hand in my direction. I shook it, and was pleased to discover that she didn't have the same grip as her husband.

"Sit down, sit down, dinner will be ready in just a few moments." She herded me towards an occupied seat and indicated for its young, male occupant to move. With a shrug and a sigh he got up and sat on the arm of the sofa. My date released her hold on me and I took his place. Her job done, Mum hurried back out of the door, presumably in the direction of the kitchen.

I was seated between the old man and the boy on the sofa arm. Grandfather twisted his body slightly as I settled into the chair next to him. His hands clasped in his lap, fingers entwined. He tilted his head on one side. "What is it you do?" he asked.

"I'm a journalist," I answered.

All eyes were still on me which added to the feeling of awkwardness. I had expected an intimate meal for two, maybe some candles, and a whispering of romantic music. Being introduced to the parents was unexpected, but being thrown headlong into a family gathering was as scary as hell.

My date had tucked her skirt and her legs underneath herself and sat on the floor in front of the fireplace.

I did a quick memory check, I was sure that it was the first date. I know that my mind had been addled by drink and drugs recently, but I'm sure I couldn't have blocked out anything else. No, I was certain it was our first time together, and that also went for the other seven. We both had different ideas about first dates, that much was clear. It was relationship acceleration beyond my comfort zone. It felt like an act of desperation on her behalf.

Maybe I was being too harsh. Perhaps she was excited about the whole thing, and had got carried away in the moment. I learned a long time ago that everyone is different and just because people do things differently, it doesn't mean they're wrong or weird. Despite that, this felt wrong, and very weird.

"Are you here to check my fanny?"

Grandmother leaned forward in her chair around her husband, looking in my direction. There was no doubt that the question had been directed at me.

"Which publication do you work for?" Grandfather enquired.

Hold on, hadn't anyone else heard that? She was still staring as if she expected an answer.

"I'm...erm...freelance."

"Any particular specialisation?" he asked.

I decided that I had misheard grandmother, but avoided looking at her anyway.

"No, I do anything. I'm easy really...said the actress to the vicar." I made the cardinal sin of laughing at my own joke; I cut it short when no-one else joined in. I looked towards my date for some sort of rescue. Her head was down and she was twirling patterns in the deep pile carpet with her fingers.

"It's my vulva you know, the carrots really chafe."

My head snapped back towards grandmother and then to the others in the room. None of them acknowledged anything had been said, and they continued to stare at me.

Discomfort had been replaced by confusion, I had no idea what was happening. I'll concede that I could've imagined the first one, but the second was definitely spoken out loud. Unless, of course I had learned to read minds. If that was the case then my new found power had picked a hell of a time to reveal itself.

Grandfather spoke again, "You must meet some interesting people."

Nowhere near as interesting as the ones I'm meeting now.

"Yes, I do. I meet some very interesting people, in fact I have an assignment today right after dinner."

"You work on a Sunday?" There was a hint of disappointment in his voice.

"Yes, I work every day if I have to."

"That's not good." Grandfather bristled. He shook his head in a way that made me feel I'd confessed I was sexually attracted to animals.

Look, I'd expected an intimate meal but I've been met by the alpha male at the door, introduced to most of my date's family. I've made a joke that no-one laughed at, and to top it off your wife is making sexual comments towards me, that only I can hear. So please don't criticise my line of work.

Grandmother stood up. "Okay doctor, get your gloves on, and make sure you get all the carrots out this time." She hitched up the hem of her skirt. I swear I glimpsed old lady pants before her husband put his hand onto her waist and gently pushed her back into her seat.

"No need for that dear, he's not the doctor," he said.

My date looked a bit sheepish."You'll have to excuse Nan, she's got dementia. We just tend to ignore her."

"Oh, that's good. No, I don't mean it's good that she's got dementia. Oh Christ, I mean it's good that I'm not mad, I thought I was hearing things...Jesus..." my sentence tailed off.

The family looked at each other. It wasn't going well. I was trying to think of something to say when a voice from outside the room yelled, "Dinner's ready!"

It was a big table, it had to be as there were eleven of us sat around it. I didn't have dinner with that many people at Christmas, let alone on a random Sunday. Grandfather was seated at the head of the table with his wife next to him, her lips moved silently as she held a conversation with herself. I sat at the opposite end of the table next to my date. They couldn't have put me any further away from them, without having built an extension.

Despite the fact I had two more meals scheduled for that afternoon, at that precise moment I was starving. I hadn't eaten all morning in preparation for my dining marathon. I'd be able to fit more food into an empty stomach.

Slices of gravy covered beef had been laid out on a serving plate, and visible wisps of aroma spiralled into the air. There were crispy Yorkshire puddings, golden brown roast potatoes, and vegetables that glistened with melted butter. It looked fantastic but the quantity was woefully inadequate for the eleven-strong team of diners.

It was reminiscent of the Serengeti wildlife programmes I had watched on television. I had to work quickly. Survival of the fittest, it was the rule of nature. The strongest got to eat, whilst the rest waited or foraged for scraps. I poised myself, my hand hovered over my fork, ready to strike.

"Right..." said grandfather.

That was the green light, and like a hunting lion striking out at a fleeing wildebeest, I pounced on the platter of beef, speared a number of slices and piled them greedily onto my plate. I congratulated myself on getting the jump on my fellow diners.

"…. let's say Grace."

Nine family members gave me a simultaneous sideways glance as they bowed their heads. Only Mad Nan ignored me, but she was busy trying to pick up the berries from the design on the table cloth.

Grandfather led them in prayer and while they had their eyes closed, I seized the opportunity to return the meat to the platter and as, "Amen" was muttered, the only evidence there had ever been anything on my plate were a few greasy skid marks, and spots of gravy splashes.

They were devoutly Christian! That explained the hostility around working on a Sunday. Oh God! I'd made the 'actress and vicar' joke, and I'd taken the lord's name in vain...twice. Three times if you counted the silent one I'd just made. I glanced around the room noticing, for the first time, the wall mounted crucifixes, baby Jesus paintings, and madonna statuettes.

At that point the one thing I remembered from my visits to Sunday school, was that the Bible recommended death by stoning for anyone found to be committing fornication. In the current situation, I am sure that Grandfather would have happily hurled the first stone, and Dad would have been waiting impatiently in the queue. I had as much chance of a sexual encounter with my date, as Judas did of being Jesus' best man.

Once everyone had served themselves, I put what was left onto my plate. A couple of very well-done roast potatoes that had been hiding at the bottom of a serving dish, the thinnest slice of meat comprising mostly of gristle, and a spoonful of mashed potato. It was a meagre helping, made even more pathetic looking by the fact I hadn't dared touch the carrots.

The family chatted amongst themselves, but I was excluded from the conversation. I'd like to think it was because I was too far away at the end of the table, but it was probably because I'd failed the, 'potential son-in-law', test at a very early stage. I was thoroughly miserable and hungry.

Dessert didn't help fill any gaps in my stomach either. A small, home-made angel cake was placed on a plate in front of each person. I waited for everyone else to start eating before I took a bite. I wasn't sure about the 'grace' business and I didn't know whether it had to be repeated at the beginning of each course.

The cake was moist and the butter icing smooth, but it was tainted with the taste of my own embarrassment. I finished the cake and folded the paper casing. I reached across the table to drop it into a small bowl as the others had done.

In making this small movement my hand hit a glass of water with such force, that I wondered why I had been moving so fast. The glass performed a spectacular dive that would have shamed a professional footballer. It landed straight on its side. Its contents spilled across the sleeve of my date and then soaked into the berries on the table-cloth.

Oh for God's sake! Just when I thought things couldn't have been any worse? Ok, four times with the 'name-in-vain' thing, but at least the last two weren't out loud.

I decided to do the gallant thing and wipe the water from the arm of my date. I delved into my pocket and whipped out the handkerchief with a flourish. Unfortunately the handkerchief was not the only thing to leave my pocket. As if it had been fired from a cannon, the emergency condom shot into the air, high above the dining table.

The conversation came to an abrupt halt.

Like the events of a car accident, everything moved in slow motion. The shiny red packet turned a few somersaults in the air. The overhead lights glinted off the metallic package making it incandescent. Then, just in case it hadn't already got everybody's attention, it maintained an eye-level altitude as it flew the length of the table. Eventually gravity grabbed it, pulling it back to earth. Landing on the table cloth, it spun and skidded to a stop perfectly placed between Grandfather and father. If it had been an Olympic gymnast, I'd have applauded.

In a panicked attempt to recover what was left of my dignity, I jumped to my feet and dashed to the head of the table, snatched up the packet, and thrust it back into the pocket of my jeans.

"I am so sorry," I said. The two men still stared at the placed where the gymnastic condom had landed, as if it had left scorch marks. In unison, they lifted their heads slowly and looked straight into my eyes. I knew they were wondering where they could find a good pointy stone.

A slight snigger from cousin was silenced with a simple look from Father. Then almost as quickly as it had stopped, the conversation continued, and I slinked back to my chair. Everybody had chosen to ignore the little indiscretion, and I was glad that Mad Nan had given them the practice in handling awkward situations.

I sat back in my chair and wished that the nightmare could be over, when suddenly someone squeezed my right thigh. It wasn't sexual, just some reassuring pressure that made me feel slightly less worried about the impression I had given my date.

Suddenly Mad Nan piped up, "Was that a rubber Johnny? I've not had one of those in years."

- TWELVE -

It had started to rain slightly when I sat back in my car. Out of sight of the house, I gripped the steering wheel at ten-to-two, and then banged my head at twelve o'clock. It was an understatement to say that the date hadn't gone well, but every cloud has a lining as shiny as a flying condom packet. There'd been no pleas for me to stay a bit longer, so I was able to leave in time to get to my next dinner date. There was also the added bonus that I was still hungry, very hungry.

The car grumbled into life when I turned the key, the wipers screamed across the windscreen, complaining that there wasn't enough rain for them to do their job properly. As I drove, I relived the dinner table moment, over and over again, and each time I winced. I'm sure I've never done anything quite so stupid.

Before heading to my next date I took a detour, via the supermarket to buy more flowers. I made sure I didn't go to the same cashier just in case she remembered me. I hoped there was no environmental reason for someone not to like flowers, because I had no idea what to buy someone with her ideals.

I checked my reflection in the car mirror for signs of stray gravy stains that would give away my earlier indiscretion with the fatty part of a beef joint. There was a spare pullover on the backseat of the car, which I slipped on. I didn't want to turn up for this date smelling like I'd just come from a house that had cooked a roast dinner.

Having checked and double checked my appearance, I popped a chewing gum in my mouth and chewed it several times, hoping it would disguise the remnants of death on my breath.

The door was opened wide before I had even reached Right-on's doorstep. Framed in the doorway, my date was dressed in baggy jeans and an over-sized t-shirt, which had a faded anti-vivisection slogan on the front. As provocative outfits went, it wasn't going to appear in the swimsuit edition of any of the magazines I'd denied writing for, but at least I wasn't under-dressed. I felt more relaxed. She stepped over the threshold and kissed me on the cheek.

"These are for you," I said, as I pushed the flowers in her dir-ection. There was a split second pause where I waited for her to say something about tearing the heart out of Mother Nature.

Her face lit up and the smile was there again. She took the flowers from me, put her nose over the top of them, and sniffed.

"They're lovely," she said.

There was no criticism, I'd made the right choice.

The hallway led to a door at the far end and she guided me into the kitchen. The smell of cooking broke through the smell of incense. It was an unmistakeable tomato aroma with a hint of herb. I guessed at a pasta sauce, which was fine by me. My stom-ach growled in anticipation.

White cabinets and wall units covered most of the space. What spare wall there was, had been painted dark red. The work surfaces were littered with all manner of cooking utensils. A waist-height fridge stood in one corner like a naughty school-boy, magnets of various colours held pieces of paper to its sur-face. There was a door in the same wall, which I assumed was a pantry.

On top of the fridge was a small tank containing a single goldfish. I couldn't help but think it was a bizarre thing to find in the house of a vegan, animal lover.

"What's with him?" I asked, pointing at the tank.

"It's not 'him', it's called 'Fish'. It's not for me to assign him a gender."

"Okay, what's with Fish?"

"It's a long story but I kind of rescued it from a fair-ground stall. It was being given away as a prize. I intended to set it free. It wasn't until I got home, that I realised that I had no idea what the natural habitat was for a goldfish.

"So I got a tank and popped it in, and Fish has been there ever since. I know it's not right to keep an animal captive, but I console myself with the thought that it'd be dead if I'd left it there. Bizarrely enough I've become quite attached."

"We're all allowed a little deviation from our beliefs every now and then," I laughed.

She went to the cooker and continued preparing our meal. Steam billowed from a couple of pans on a gas hob at the other end. I walked towards the cooking pots.

"No, no," she wagged her finger, "it's a surprise. I hope you like a bit of variety."

"Man cannot live by bread alone," I said.

"A 'person' cannot live by bread alone," she corrected.

"Oh, yes of course."

She pointed me towards a table that was shoved against the back wall which, considering it was broad daylight, was pointlessly lit by a small candle. The place mats were mis-matched, and the knives and forks had lost contact with their identical twins long ago. Single sheets of paper towel had been folded into triangles, and slotted into two wine glasses. It wasn't the Ritz, but I could see that she had really tried to make it look special, and she had succeeded. It had been a long time since anyone had tried to impress me, and I felt a tingling of happiness.

"Excuse my back," she said as she turned towards the cooker.

"Don't worry," I entertained myself watching the vague outline of the jean-clad buttocks, that peeked out from beneath the extra large t-shirt.

"Have you been busy?" She didn't look up from the pans.

"No, not really." It was hot in the kitchen, so I slipped off my pullover and hung it over the back of one of the chairs.

"Oh, I thought you said you had a job this morning."

The receptionist was right, keeping tabs on your own lies wasn't easy.

"I thought you meant today. I only had one job this morning so I haven't been busy today."

"Is that a good or bad thing?"

"Bad if I need the money. Good if I get to spend time doing things like this."

She turned and smiled; another point for me.

I studied her back in silence for a few minutes, and not just her buttocks. If I ignored the veganism, hyper-politically correctness, and the fact that she dressed like a tree-hugging bypass hater, she was perfect.

"Are you busy the rest of the time?"

"It varies, but sometimes there's too much work for one man."

"Person," she said.

"Sorry?"

"Too much work for one person."

"Yes, that's what I meant." But that's not what I meant, I was referring to me, and I'm a man.

"Help yourself to wine," she said.

The bottle on the table had already been uncorked, and I assumed that it had been left to breathe, only because I thought that's what wine was supposed to do. I relieved one of the glasses of its makeshift napkin, and replaced it with some of the pink liquid from the bottle.

"Are you having one?" I asked.

She shook her head. "Not at the moment."

I lifted the glass and examined the contents. Perhaps she was hoping to get me drunk so that she could have her wicked way with me. Damn, why had I brought the car? A little bit of liquid inhibition was exactly what I needed. Mind you, it wouldn't go down well if I turned up to my parent's house in a drunken mess.

I swirled the glass and took a swig. My taste buds immediately screamed loudly in protest, and I held the liquid in my mouth, too frightened to swallow. I looked around desperately for some sort of receptacle that I could spit it into. No plant pots, no bowls, no buckets.

The situation became urgent, there was no doubt in my mind that the liquid was corrosive, and I could already feel it eating through my cheeks. I checked the label on the bottle to make sure I hadn't accidentally taken a drink of bleach. For a moment I thought about re-filling the bottle but decided that would be wrong.

"You okay?" She asked without looking at me.

"Mmmmm." It was all I could manage in the circumstances.

"How's the wine?" She still hadn't turned around.

There was nothing for it, I had to act before my teeth started to dissolve. I side-stepped across to the fridge, and in one swift move, covered by the noise of hissing steam and clattering pot lids, I spat the wine into the fish tank.

"Lovely," I said. If the gap between her question and my answer had been too long, she didn't say anything.

I took a sharp intake of breath trying to cool the sensation.

"It's brewed by a small tribe in the Amazon rain-forests. It's made from different berries and roots gathered by the villagers. It's got an unusual taste don't you think?"

"Yes, really unusual." I stuck my tongue out and waved my hand furiously over it, trying to get as much cool air as possible into my mouth.

"It's a bit of an acquired taste, but it's good to know that just by buying a bottle I'm helping the less fortunate."

Less fortunate? They were definitely more fortunate seeing as they probably didn't drink the stuff. My tongue stung as I ran it around the inside of my mouth. The insides of my cheeks were rough and wrinkled, having had all the moisture sapped from them.

I picked up the bottle and examined the label. A brightly coloured bird mocked me from the safety of the branch of a tree in a jungle, several thousands of miles away. Apparently this '*quirky*' little number was brewed by the Crupilupi tribe in the depths of the Amazon rainforest. Made from berries and root tuber to an ancient recipe handed down through time, and kept a secret amongst the tribesmen. A tribe untouched by civilisation.

Not that untouched if they had access to glass bottles, and the means to print labels.

A glance at the fish tank told me that the aquatic connoisseur was none the worse for the wine-tasting experience.

"It's almost ready," said my hostess, "sit yourself down."

The chair scraped along the floor as I pulled it out and dropped myself into it. I chose the seat facing the fridge, which meant that I could keep an eye on the tank-dweller.

Right-on brought two large plates to the table and placed them on the mats. She went back to the cooker and retrieved the largest pan. Having placed it on the table, she ladled some of its contents onto my plate.

When the steam had cleared, I got my first good look at my dinner. She had served up white pebbles and gravel, in a tomato sauce.

She must have seen my confused look.

"Butterbean and lentil casserole," she announced proudly as she filled her own plate.

If you had asked me to describe my nightmare meal, then this would not have been far from it. All it needed was a few peas and sweetcorn, and it would've been gastronomic hell.

"Lovely," I lied.

She swapped the pans and returned to the table where she liberally sprinkled further misery onto my plate, in the form of the aforementioned, dreaded vegetables. Oh God!

She sat down. "Don't stand on ceremony, tuck in."

What a dilemma. The woman had slaved over a hot stove and produced a meal fit for a Buddhist monk, and I was ungrateful. She had already started eating and the pressure was on. There was no way I could get away with not eating it without causing major offence. I was after all a vegetarian, and she probably assumed this was my staple diet.

I passed the fork through the mixture and scooped up a couple of beans and some lentils. As I brought them closer to my mouth, the smooth surface of the pulses reminded me of the shell of a large albino insect.

Using all my powers of coercion I got the fork past my lips and into my mouth. I argued silently with my jaw, trying to convince it that closing would be a good thing. It knew I was lying, but gave in anyway.

Tomato sauce settled in my mouth and left little solid objects on my tongue. I thought about swallowing the mouthful straight away, but it would have ended badly. Probably with coughing, choking, Heimlich manoeuvres, and maybe an ambulance. As an exit strategy, it didn't seem such a bad option, but I couldn't bring myself to do it.

The sensation of chewing on a butterbean was how I imagined it would be if I bit down on a dung beetle. The texture was gross and I stifled a wretch before it became obvious. I chewed again and this time the lentils exploded in my mouth, like tiny blackhead spots releasing their puss.

I chewed, forcing the contents to the back of my throat and swallowed quickly. I reached for the wine glass in order to wash it down, and stopped just short of the stem. The wine would just make matters worse.

Across the table, Right-on was making good work of demolishing her food.

She looked over her poised fork. "Everything ok?" she asked.

"Mmmm, lovely," I lied…again.

"I must admit I make this quite a lot. It is quite easy to do and I love the flavours. Do you have any favourites?"

Beef, pork, lamb, chicken! For Christ's sake anything but this vomit-inducing concoction.

"Not really, I'll try most things." Which is true but I've always made it a personal rule never to eat food that looks the same coming out as it does going in, whichever end it emerged from.

I had only myself to blame, this woman thought I was a vegetarian and had cooked up something she thought I would like. What did I think I was going to be served? It was never going to be meat. Things were so bad, I would even put up with the cardboard meat substitute, made popular by the wives of elderly pop-stars.

My heart sank as I stared at the insurmountable pile of dog

puke on my plate. I had to come up with a plan to make the food disappear, which didn't involve actually eating it. There was no way I was going to clear the plate, and dropping it into the fish tank would definitely not go unnoticed.

They say that necessity is the mother of invention, and in this case the father had been panic. I hatched a plan in haste without fully thinking it through. I pulled myself a little closer to the table. I used my left hand and pulled the hem of my T-shirt over my thighs, this formed an improvised bib across my lap. I took a large forkful of food and lifted it towards my mouth, when I was sure that Right-on was not looking in my direction, and I was obscured by the pans on the table, I tipped the food directly into my lap, and caught it in my t-shirt. Pure genius!

I continued in this manner until she had eaten her serving. I still had some food left on my plate, but I feigned being full.

"Finished?" she asked.

"Yes, thanks. I couldn't eat another mouthful." Which wasn't a complete lie.

She reached across for my plate. "Are you sure, you don't want any more?"

Under the table I still clutched the hem of my T-shirt with one hand, I waved her away with the other. "Definitely not, thank you though, it was lovely."

"Good, I'm glad you liked it. I'll do it again if you're nice to me." She stood up and walked towards the sink.

"I'll give you a hand with the washing, but I could do with using your toilet first."

She turned back to face me still holding the plates in one hand, with the other on her hip, "I do hope that's not a comment about my cooking." She cocked her head on one side and smiled, then she turned and dropped the plates into the sink.

"No, no. Of course not, it was great."

I made the assumption that the toilet would be upstairs. I jumped to my feet and nursing the slop that rested against my stomach, rather than in it, I headed for the door.

She called after me as I left, but in my haste I didn't hear what she said. She laughed and then shouted, "It doesn't matter."

Once out of sight, I tried not to lose any of the contents of my T-shirt, whilst I hurried as quickly as I could along the hallway and up the stairs. I found the bathroom without any spillage. I shut, and locked the door behind me.

I knelt down in front of the toilet and lifted the seat. The noise that accompanied the pouring of the concoction again reminded me of vomit. I used my hands and brushed the more stubborn pieces from the T-shirt, leaving a large orange stain. Why the hell had I chosen to wear white?

Some of the stain disappeared with the vigorous rubbing of handfuls of tissue paper, but it was still very visible. I stripped to the waist and turned the tap on. I held the stained part of the T-shirt under the running water, and tried to keep the rest of it dry. There was a few seconds where the water ran orange, but then it stopped. I rubbed the cloth as hard as I could, again there was a short burst of discoloured water, before the water ran clear again. I looked around the room for something to use as a detergent. I was willing to give anything a try. In a panic, I applied all manner of liquids to the stain in the hope that something would work. Unfortunately everything was ethically sourced and I doubted any of it would have even cleaned mud off a mirror.

Once I had wrung the T-shirt out as best I could, I put it back on, tucking the hem of the T-shirt into the front of my trousers and pushing it down as far as I could. The eight inch wide orange stain was unmissable, it looked like the sun was setting in my pants.

I then had a bright idea, I turned the T-shirt back to front. The stain would then be at the back and less likely to be seen. I looked in the full length mirror, the thought of Right-on having been stood naked in front of this mirror flashed through my mind, before I realised that the stain was still highly visible. There were two options, either I avoided turning my back to her, or I found something to cover it with. Wait! I had a pullover. Unfortunately it was on the back of a chair in the kitchen.

I needed to get back downstairs. I'd been gone for some time, she could come scouting for me at any moment.

My mission was to get that pullover. I unlocked the door and was about to open it, when my eye caught the un-flushed toilet bowl, or more accurately its contents.

I had seen toilets like that before but it was usually after copious amounts of alcohol had been imbibed. I muttered a silent prayer to whichever being had made me look that direction before leaving.

I pushed the lever and waited. There was a slight trickle, which hardly disturbed the surface of the water in the bowl before it stopped. I worked the lever again hoping that I hadn't pressed it hard enough the first time. The result was the same and the butterbeans bobbed defiantly.

Further desperate yanks on the lever only resulted in hollow, metal clunking sounds. I grabbed the toilet brush and started stabbing at the bowl, trying to break up the contents enough for them to be affected by the water that dribbled out from the cistern. I flushed and stabbed, and stabbed and flushed. Each time a little more of the contents slipped away, but it was going to take forever. I snatched a small mug from the sink and removed the toothbrush it was holding. I filled it with water from the tap and poured it into the toilet bowl. It worked, but only very slightly. I did this several times until a thin but lumpy soup remained. It would have to do. I took a few sheets of toilet paper and laid them down carefully on top of the water, in the hope that it would hide the contents. Maybe Right-on was one of those people who never looked into the toilet, and I'd be safe.

She was stood near the sink when I returned to the kitchen. I quickly grabbed my pullover and tied it around my waist.

"Can I help?" I asked.

"You can dry these few pots if you'd be so kind." She threw me a tea towel and I started to help.

"You were gone a while, everything ok?"

"Er, yes, er, fine. Just had a bit of a problem with the, er..."

"Flush?"

"Yes, the flush."

"It can be a bit troublesome. I had an eco water system installed. It helps reduce my water consumption and my impact on the environment, but it does take some getting used to."

Troublesome? That didn't really describe it. I wondered how a woman who's diet consisted solely of vegetables and other roughage, managed to get rid of her own personal waste. Maybe she didn't dispose of them through the toilet, perhaps she carried her lady-logs out into the garden where she made her own compost.

She went off onto some diatribe about polar icecaps, global warming, and the water table, whilst I tried to get rid of the image my last thought had put into my head. An accidental glance at the fish tank showed the occupant swimming in rather a strange manner. Fish was swaying from side to side in what can only be described as the goldfish equivalent of a drunken stagger. When it bumped into the glass side, it visibly shook its head and set of staggering in the other direction.

Right-on finished washing and when I'd dried the last item she took it off me and put it away in a cupboard.

"Do you want any dessert?"

"No, that would be greedy," I said. In reality I didn't want to risk being fed sweet bat guano in a strawberry jus.

"Coffee then?" she asked.

"Yes please."

"Make yourself at home in the living room and I'll bring it in to you."

In the living room I sank into the sofa and allowed my eyes to adjust to the red-hued darkness. I had only been in the room once before and hadn't realised that there was no television. A room looks strange without a least a 42" flat screen, like it's been burgled. I did a quick check on the footprint of the house from memory. It was the only ground floor room other than the kitchen, so there was no television downstairs. As I looked around to see what else was missing, Right-on walked into the room carrying two cups and handed me one.

"Not comfortable?" she asked.

I was seated right on the edge of the seat, because to sit back meant the T-shirt pressed against the cushions and made everything it touched wet. I'd have a problem explaining the dark patches that appeared.

"I'm fine, thanks."

She sat down on one of the armchairs and tucked her legs underneath her. "You look nervous, I'm not going to bite," she said.

She was a vegetarian, there was no chance that would have happened, however much I wanted it to. Oh God! She didn't bite...a sudden disappointing, and inappropriate possibility shot through my head, but I didn't allow it to stay.

"You don't eat any meat?" I asked.

She looked puzzled, "No, none. What about you?"

Another opportunity presented itself to come clean. Lying was no basis for a relationship. I looked at her, curled snuggly against the arm of the chair, clutching a coffee cup. Her hair was slightly tousled and that baggy t-shirt, that gave just a hint of curve, made her look shabby-sexy. I was convinced that my yearning for this woman would be a distant memory, if I told her everything now. Besides, the pause whilst I thought about what to say was suspicious.

"Not really."

"Not really," she repeated, "what does that mean?" She leaned forward slightly.

Think quick, think quick. "It means that I did once but I had a change of heart a while ago." About the time I met you to be exact.

This relaxed her, and she settled back into her chair. "Me too. It took some time to convince my parents that I was serious. I told them during a Sunday dinner. Mum had cooked a huge roast beef joint, with potatoes, veg, and meat gravy. When I didn't eat the meat they asked why. I told them I was a vegetarian. They thought I was going through some sort of fad, but eventually they caved in. I haven't eaten meat since I was about 13."

Roast beef, potatoes, meat gravy! I felt hungry, so hungry. I nodded in agreement, and tried to adjust my position so that she couldn't hear the noises that had started echoing through my stomach. I sat back in the chair hoping a different sitting position would stop the growling. I immediately regretted the move as I felt the cold, wetness of my T-shirt.

To cover any facial expressions I took a drink of coffee. How I wish I hadn't taken such a big gulp. Quite apart from it being scalding hot, the coffee had clearly been made by the same un-civilised tribe as the wine.

She noticed the look on my face. "Is everything ok?" she asked.

"Sugar," I said.

She jumped up and headed to the kitchen and returned with a small bowl. I slipped two heaped spoonfuls into the cup and rested it in my lap. She put her own cup on the coffee table and sat down next to me. The sofa was small and one side of her body pressed against mine. She placed a hand on my thigh, the shiver that ran through my body almost made me spill the contents of the coffee cup.

She pushed herself closer to me and I felt the softness of her right breast as it pressed against my upper arm, she leaned her head on my shoulder. Her fingernails raked along the fabric of my jeans and she gave a cute little shrug of her shoulders. It was a long time since I had been in such an intimate position with a woman, and I didn't want to move. I liked the feeling. I wanted to put my cup down, but I judged the distance to the coffee table as being too far to lean without ruining the position we were in, and I was concerned that we'd never get it back. I luxuriated in the closeness and the pleasant feelings that were coursing through my body.

Then I realised that there were stirrings in my lap that had nothing to do with the cup this time, and the more I tried not to think about it, the more things started to feel uncomfortable.

I had one hand trapped between us whilst the other held the

cup. I couldn't adjust my trousers to give myself some 'growing' room.

I turned my head to look at her and she looked directly at me. She took the turn of my head as an indication and moved in slowly, pressing her lips to mine. There was no urgency, just the smallest amount of pressure and a tender, gentleness. There wasn't the battling tongues or the exchange of saliva that I'd experienced with Hamster-Chick, and thankfully there was no taste of cigarettes. This was not some porn film snog, but a romantic, old movie style kiss. I mimicked her kissing style as best as I could. I barely grazed her lips with mine, I tried not to show any sense of urgency and I focussed on the task. I turned my head at the right time to avoid nose clashes. When did kissing become so difficult?

My mind might have been occupied, but certain other parts of my body had taken a full interest in the events, and I tried to sink into the settee to make my 'interest' less obvious.

The longer the kiss went on the more my mind wandered and I became aware of other things. The arm that was trapped between us tingled with the start of pins and needles, the dampness of the t-shirt on my back, and the heat of the coffee cup which penetrated the fabric of my trousers. I moved to get into position that would alleviate my discomfort.

She took this as a cue to move things to the next level and seized hold of the hem of my T-shirt closest to her, and started to pull it out of my waistband. I needed to keep my stained T-shirt hidden. As I twisted slightly and tried to stop her, she stretched her other hand across my body to grab the other side.

That's when it all went wrong!

The hand that reached across my body collided heavily with the almost full cup of scalding, foul-tasting coffee. The cup upturned and deposited its lava temperature contents directly into my lap. There was a split second of stillness while the liquid soaked through the fabric of my jeans, and then my underwear. Right-On recoiled in shock when she realised what had happened and I jumped to my feet, dropping the cup on the floor where it smashed. I unfastened my belt and started to re-move my jeans when I realised that I was not in an appropriate, physical state to get naked in front of a woman, so I ran upstairs unfastening my buttons as I went. I slammed and locked the bathroom door. I stripped off and splashed myself with water.

There was reddening, but nothing that would need skin grafts. I started putting my wet clothes back on, when there was a tap on the bathroom door.

"Are you okay?" she asked from outside.

"I'm fine, just a little sore."

"Is everything ok…you know, down there?"

"My manhood is intact."

"Penis."

"What?"

"Penis, not manhood," she said.

It really wasn't the time for lessons in political correctness.

I was fully dressed when I opened the door. She threw her arms around me. "I'm so sorry."

"It wasn't your fault, it was an accident. I think I need to go home and get changed."

We went to the front door and hugged again.

"I'm so sorry. Please call me."

I kissed her forehead. "I will."

As I walked down the path, I looked like a cowboy with haemorrhoids.

- THIRTEEN -

In addition to the slight burning sensation in my groin, I was sporting the frustrated ache of a courting teenager. I had briefly stopped at home to change clothes.

As I let myself into my parents' address, I slipped into 'son' mode.

"It's only me," I shouted.

There was a muffled greeting from somewhere down the hall. A wall of heat and steam hit me when I pushed open the kitchen door. Mum was hunched over several pots on the cooker, the combination of smells was amazing.

"Hello sweetheart," she said. She leaned her head towards me as she stirred the contents of the pans. I dutifully planted a kiss on the offered cheek.

"Are you hungry?"

"Oh God yes, I'm starving," I said, while lifting he lids on the pan and inhaling the smell of the contents.

She shooed me away from the cooker. "Good, it shouldn't be long now. Your Dad's in the living room, go and keep him company."

Leaving her to the cooking, I went to find Dad. He was sat in his usual place; the single-seater armchair, next to the fire and with a direct, unobstructed view of the television, which was in the very rare state of being switched off. There was a pile of newspapers on the floor next to him at his feet. I saw that the colour supplements had all been surgically removed and dumped in the waste paper bin.

He had one paper open and held out at arm's length in front of him. He refused to go to the opticians to have his eyesight reassessed, so he worked with a prescription that was about ten years old. He also wore bifocals which meant he had to tilt his head backwards. It looked incredibly uncomfortable, but it was the only way he could focus on the print.

I walked in and sat on the sofa. "Afternoon father," I said.

"Hmmph!" He grunted and shook the paper out, but didn't look at me.

"Have you been busy?" I asked. He turned his head slightly and looked out the corner of his eyes. He'd been retired for six years, so I knew he was never busy. He split his time evenly between the garden and the armchair.

"Are you responsible for any of this crap?" he said and jabbed the page with his finger.

Sometimes I was lucky and a big daily newspaper would take up one of my stories, and I'd get a bit of extra cash.

"Not this week. The nationals aren't interested in garden fetes."

"Crap! Crap! Crap!" He punctuated each word with an aggressive turn of a page.

"And yet you continue to buy every paper, every week."

He grunted again. "Bunch of nosy, immoral vultures."

The comment was aimed at me. He had never approved of my career choice. In fact if anyone ever asked what his son did for a living, he'd say I was in prison because he didn't want people to think he'd failed as a parent.

I distinctly remembered the talk he'd given to the teenage me, about my future. Once he had successfully destroyed any dreams I had of becoming a racing driver or a fighter pilot, he'd set about planning my future.

He had a specific idea what I should do. I should learn a trade and then spend the rest of my life in the same sort of dead-end job as he had. I had seen the effect that 30 years in a 'secure trade' had on his personality, and I didn't want to go down that road. I wanted to do something more than walk up and down a warehouse floor checking off stock on a clipboard.

"So, let's be realistic. What would you like to do?" He had asked. It had sounded like I had options.

Looking back, I should have stood up to him. I should have been more forceful and stuck to my dreams, but there and then under the interrogation of my father, I buckled and my career lorry jack-knifed on the road to Dream Job Land.

"Teacher?" I'd offered.

"Lazy scum."

"Err…Advertising executive?"

"Lying scum."

"Uhm…Journalist?"

"Immoral scum."

"I…I…I don't know then," I'd stuttered.

"Well, you'd better have a think and it had better be something useful and productive."

By 'useful' he'd meant 'boring', and by 'productive' he'd meant 'repetitive'. And it would probably have included wearing a hard-hat.

I spent my school and college life having no idea what I'd be doing as an adult. It was a number of years later that I spoke to a careers advisor, who made me take a test aimed at determining the profession that would best suit me. I had answered all questions and was told I should be a journalist and, despite my Dad's open disgust and protests, that's what happened. My working life was determined on the answers given in a questionnaire.

As a result I had always been a disappointment and he never passed up the opportunity to let me know it. In my own way I had come to accept that I would never live up to his low standards, and his comments no longer caused me any distress. My Dad loved me, he wanted the best, but he wanted it to be on his terms.

We performed the same verbal dance each time I saw him and I knew that at any minute he would start with the…

"Your brother got it right, he got himself a proper job."

Ah, right on cue. My younger brother, the golden child. Works as a bank administrator, married to a well-paid, city lawyer. Big house somewhere in the suburbs, 2.4 children, a dog, and a gas-guzzling prestige car parked in the drive. Apparently that's the definition that appeared next to the word 'successful' in my Dad's dictionary.

Parents aren't supposed to have favourites, but it's clear that mine did. The walls of their home were full of photographs of the happy little family; brother on his own, brother and Lawyer, brother with the two children, Beelzebub and Lucifer, and the devil's spawn on their own. The combinations were endless, add the dog into the mix and they were almost infinite. I think somewhere in the house was a picture of me and if my memory serves me right it was in the downstairs toilet.

During childhood, I was grounded if I got home 30 seconds after my curfew. My brother could waltz in three hours late, clutching an empty bottle of cider, and my parents wouldn't even bat an eyelid. When I challenged the inequality of our treatment, I was told that as a parent you learned with your first child, and tried not to make similar mistakes with the second. So I was a prototype!

My adventurous brother ribbed me mercilessly about my lifestyle. Whilst he walked barefoot up Mount Kilimanjaro, I was having afternoon tea with two of Tin-man's boring friends. He reminded me that he had been skydiving out of a plane whilst I had been at the local DIY store, choosing bedroom wallpaper. He said that my comfortable relationship made me dull.

When your younger sibling takes the limelight and your parents already appear disappointed in you, the pressure is off.

Whilst staring at the newspaper, he treated me to a run down of my brother's life to date, and the successes of the devil children at their respective extra-curricular activities. I wondered whether he was regaled with tales of my personal successes, about my visits to council meetings, and supermarket openings. Somehow I doubted it.

They'd have had a discussion about my relationship breakup. Dad would have said I'd failed at something else, my brother would have said it was the most exciting thing to have happened in my life, and Mum would have been happy as she'd never liked Tin-man.

Dad continued his diatribe and I tuned him out, nodding occasionally in the hope that he thought I was listening. When it went silent I gathered he'd finished.

"How's the garden?" I asked in order to fill the silence.

"Hedgehogs," he replied.

"Sorry," I said. "Is that some non-offensive swear word you've invented?"

"Bloody hedgehogs, bloody nuisance," He stared straight at the newspaper.

"I though they were the gardener's friend. I wrote a piece for a gardening magazine once about how useful they were in ridding the garden of pests."

"Hmmphh!" he grunted, "pointless, flea-ridden vermin."

At that point mum walked into the the room with several plates balanced along her arms like a professional silver service waitress. "Don't stroke Spartacus, he's got fleas," she warned.

So that was it, my Dad's beloved pedigree Persian cat had caught fleas, and he blamed it on a hedgehog.

The fact that the animal got up close and personal with anything on four legs and could have been infested by any one of a thousand neighbourhood creatures, had clearly escaped his attention. My Dad's refusal to have him neutered because he might want to breed him one day, meant that he had fathered enough kittens for a remake of 'The Aristocats'.

The gently purring, show-standard feline lay majestically on the windowsill, looking every bit as elegant and royal as his family tree suggested. You'd never have thought that this was the same animal that had been shot with a tranquilliser gun by the vet when, overcome with sexual desire, it had chased the next door neighbour's Doberman half a mile to the park and then cornered it behind the children's play area.

Mum placed the dishes on the already set table at the rear of the room. Dad and I took our seats while mum ferried back and forth.

"Don't wait for me, tuck in," she said.

There was no prayer and there was plenty to go around. I

didn't have to hide at the end of the table hoping I wasn't seen, and I didn't embarrass myself by throwing a condom across the table.

I was so grateful to be eating food that didn't resemble insects that I stuffed myself to bursting point, and then had some more. It was so long since I had eaten anything decent. When I finally couldn't swallow another morsel, I sat back in the chair and patted my distended stomach.

"That was awesome, mum."

"Fantastic as always," said Dad. He tipped some wine into each of our glasses. He picked his up, swilled it around, and then held the rim underneath his nose. He must've seen it on a television programme somewhere because he knew nothing about wine. He held his glass up in a toast.

"Here's to swimming with bow-legged women."

I smiled, it was his standard salute.

My phone beeped as a message came through.

- Hope you're having fun and haven't slipped up

It was the Receptionist.

- Not as easy as I thought it would be. Fill you in when I see you

- Ok. X -

"So are you courting yet?" Mum asked. Even though she knew I had recently separated and still smarted from the pain, she needed to know about my love life.

Well, I've had two dinner dates before I came to you, one with a vegetarian and the other with a God-groupie. I collected an entire plate of bean stew in my t-shirt, before sustaining minor burns to my manhood…sorry penis, and I also threw a contraceptive at some potential in-laws. I'm not sure whether I should see either of them again. Oh, and there's the small matter of being arrested after taking illegal drugs. You'd be so proud of me.

"Sort of," I replied.

"What's that supposed to mean?" she said.

"It's kind of complicated."

"He's gay," Dad said, as he examined the liquid in his glass

"I'm not gay, Dad. It's just that my options have become, well plentiful."

"He's bisexual, doubling his chances."

"Dad, I'm not bisexual. I'm just in a difficult position."

"Doesn't sound like you're getting into any positions to me." He smirked and emptied his wine glass with one swallow.

Mum gave him a hard stare.

"I'm not entirely sure what's happening myself, but as soon as I know I'll tell you."

"You're not thinking of having that woman back are you?" Mum asked.

The mention of Tin-man sent a pang of sadness through me. I remembered how many times we'd had a Sunday dinner at this very table, usually right after having visited a local garden centre to buy some new window boxes.

"Oh no, that's the last thing I would ever do." Although at that moment, I wasn't entirely sure. All the time I had spent mourning my loss seemed a waste. I obviously still had feelings for her, and I missed the life we shared. I tried to remember the last time I had thought about her and I couldn't pin-point it, but the sense of loss was still there.

"Good, she's bad news that one. I said that right from the start." She wagged her finger as she spoke.

"And who did you say this to, Mum, because it wasn't me?"

The wagging finger stopped. "I told your Dad, didn't I?" She looked at him, but he was engrossed in his wine glass.

"Why didn't you say anything to me?" I asked.

"Well sometimes you need to make your own mistakes; it's the only way you'll learn."

"But it's not a very pleasant way to learn," I said. "How about next time you just tell me you when think it's wrong?"

"And have you hate me?"

"I would never hate you, Mum."

"Maybe not but you wouldn't believe me. No, you need to find these things out for yourself."

"I don't know how to find out. How do you know when things are right, when you've found the right one?"

Mum looked at Dad who turned his wine glass by the stem, lost in his own little world.

"When there are no secrets and you know everything about each other," she said.

Dad let out a huge burp then followed it up by tipping his body weight onto one buttock, and farting.

"And nothing that person does makes you embarrassed."

- FOURTEEN -

The following morning I laid in bed and stared at the ceiling, I knew that I should be up and working, but I took a few minutes to take stock of my life. I'm not entirely sure how I'd managed to end up where I was. Don't get me wrong, I'm not complaining, having three women interested in me gave my ego a much needed boost.

If the previous day had taught me anything, it was that three women meant three times the problems. I had to remember where I was meant to be, when I was supposed to be there, who I was meeting, and most importantly, who I was. Juggling three women was hard.

All three relationships were in their early stages, and I had to make a decision about which one to stick with. I couldn't decide as I hadn't spent a great deal of time with any of them. I thought about each of them and tried to decide on which one I should concentrate my efforts.

Right-on was in the lead. After two dates, she was the one that I knew most about. She was gorgeous, definitely the best looking of the three. She was the easiest to talk to, as long as I ignored the constant amendments to my political incorrectness. The subject matter was sometimes a little too 'hippy', but I liked her. She could be long-term girlfriend material, but there was the issue of the veganism. Could people with two different diets co-exist as a partnership? I'm sure they could. Maybe I would have to change and forego meat altogether. It would be a massive change to my lifestyle, but lots of people make changes in the name of love. Some even change religion.

Speaking of religion, there was God-groupie. She was attractive and physically fit, there was also the added plus point that I hadn't lied to her. I didn't know a huge amount about her; the family dinner date hadn't given us much opportunity to chat.

I was worried about the religious aspect to her life. I'm not sure I could commit in the way that she had done. For the man who had been without a girlfriend for a couple of months, the biggest drawback was the unlikelihood of sex, without the wedding being held first.

The family were another concern. It wasn't just the hostility of Father, but the speed with which it had happened. I'd always thought that meeting the parents should be left for later in a relationship. The rate at which things had moved made me feel uncomfortable. In fact it wasn't discomfort, it was outright fear. I needed another opportunity to make a proper assessment.

And finally, there was Hamster-Chick, she had an indefinable something that made her attractive. From what my alcohol fogged brain can remember, she was a fun, party animal. So what if she smoked and took drugs? She ate meat and worshipped nothing other than dance music. There was the small issue that I had taken ten years off my age, but maybe I could tell her she'd misheard, or perhaps convince her that the drugs had caused memory problems.

If any of the three were going to be up for sex, it was her. A woman with her levels of energy had needs and would no doubt be insatiable. She was my best bet for a physical relationship.

Is that what it all came down to? Sex? I can't deny that it was important, particularly as I laid in bed alone. I needed the stability and comfort that I thought I'd had in my previous relationship. I also wanted the physical benefits, so yes it was partly about the sex.

It was difficult to choose between them, and I figured that I didn't have enough information in order to make a decision on any future partner. I decided to assess each one before I selected the right candidate for the post. It would be like an extended recruitment process, and the selection procedure would continue with further dates to gather evidence.

Hamster-chick was the first of my re-interviews. It was a while since I had seen her and she was probably wondering whether I was ever going to get in touch. She had left me her number which meant she wanted to see me again. I owed it to her to make contact.

I reached for my phone and I was scrolling through the contacts, looking for her number, when it chirped into life and a text message appeared.

- Got a job for you. Get your sweet ass here now. X

It was the Receptionist. I couldn't afford the luxury of turning down work so I typed an 'OK' and pressed send.

I decided against ringing Hamster-chick and chose the coward's way. I sent a text and asked if we could meet up again. I climbed out of bed, before I'd even reached the bathroom she replied telling me to meet her at work that afternoon. That would give me enough time to get whatever job the Receptionist had for me completed, before going straight out to meet her.

I washed and dressed and, after optimistically securing the acrobatic condom in my wallet, left the house with a spring in my step.

The spring had turned into a bounce by the time I entered the newspaper office. I threw myself into a swivel chair which spun with my momentum. After a couple of turns I stopped it facing the computer screen. I leaned forward to press the power button, when a mug of coffee appeared over my shoulder and landed on the desk in front of me.

"White, two sugars?" said the Receptionist.

"That's great, thanks."

She made her way to the desk on the opposite side.

"So, how's the love life?" she asked.

"Still complicated."

"Still?" She sounded surprised.

"I can't go on like this, I've got to make a decision about which one I'm sticking with."

"Which one is it then?"

"That's just it, I don't know how to decide."

"How about you put them all in a ring, and the last one standing wins your heart?" she laughed.

"In jelly or oil?"

She tilted her head and looked up for a second. "I'm not sure, it's your future, you decide. Personally I'd go for custard, it tastes so much better."

"I like your thinking, but I'm going to see them all again before I make a decision."

"Like a job interview?"

"No, it's not like that. I need to know more about them."

"More like an audition then. Which one is leading at the moment?'

"I don't know. I'm seeing the girl I met in the pub later, so I'll see how it goes."

"Is she the favourite?" she asked.

"Maybe," I said.

"Even though she got you drunk, gave you drugs, and then disappeared while you got arrested?"

"I guess."

"It's not the most encouraging start to a long term relationship,' she said.

"No, but it's a story we'll be able to tell our kids."

"Wow, it must be serious if you're thinking that far ahead"

"I'm not, I'm only thinking as far as the next date and maybe the chance..." I stopped.

"The chance of what?"

I didn't answer, I didn't have to.

"Oh, I get it now, it's all about sex. Typical man," she said, rolling her eyes.

"No it's not about sex," I lied, "it's a confusing situation. I thought that if I kept my options open then I could pick the one best suited to me. I want a girlfriend and this is currently the best plan I have."

"Maybe you're trying a bit too hard to find love. Don't go

looking and it might find you."

I sighed, "I didn't go looking last week and it found me... three times."

"That's not love," she laughed again. "Look, just be careful."

She reached into a tray at the side of the desk and slid a couple of stapled sheets of paper across to me. Clipped to the front was a cutting from another newspaper, "There's today's mission. Good luck Mr. Bond." She stood up and walked to her own desk.

"Thanks Moneypenny," I called after her. I studied the papers, I was off to cover the wedding of a 85-year-old man and his 83-year-old girlfriend; not an anniversary, an actual wedding.

It wasn't a difficult assignment. I watched the ceremony from the back of the church, and wondered whether the vicar had brought along his funeral notes...just in case. Macro Mike took a couple of photos. If nothing else we could always hang on to the pictures for their respective obituaries.

The reception was held at their care home, which was a short shuffle from the church. I caught up with them in the faintly scented community room. They'd been childhood sweethearts; separated, lived two completely separate lives until the death of their respective spouses left them single again. They met up, rekindled their love, and got married. It was heartwarming, it gave me hope that anyone could find love, but I didn't want to wait until I was an octogenarian.

Throughout the job, my mind was preoccupied with my date. As I left the elderly lovebirds to their reception and wedding night, I thought about where I would take Hamster Chick. I was concerned that she'd have plans for some activity and I would be unable to keep up. I took the initiative and suggested a quiet drink and a meal.

When I'd found a parking space, I reached into the glove compartment and retrieved a bottle of aftershave. I gave myself a quick squirt to hide the lingering smell of old people, checked my reflection for any signs of my real age, and made my way into the pub.

Hamster-Chick was busy serving a group of young men and she didn't see me when I entered. I perched myself on a stool at the opposite end of the bar. I watched the interaction. She won them over with that sparkling smile.

I noticed the odd admiring glance at her cleavage, and I could have sworn that she pushed her chest out just a little bit further than usual. They all stared when she bent down and fetched bottles from the fridge behind her and I thought she lingered longer than necessary.

She took their money, gave them their change with a wink, and they wandered off to find a seat, no doubt discussing their chances with the barmaid who they'd left wiping the bar. She suddenly caught sight of me, threw down the towel she'd been holding, and skipped over. She put both hands on the bar and used it to lift herself towards me. She gave me a quick, cigarette-tainted, kiss on the lips, dropped back down, and looked at her watch.

The group she'd served had seen me and I was now the sad boyfriend keeping an eye on his working girlfriend.

"Just ten more minutes jailbird," she said. She moved to a pump, poured a pint and dropped it in front of me.

I eyed the pint with a degree of suspicion, it had been the road to ruin last time. I vowed to take things slower and remain sober. I needed to remember the date if I had to compare her to the others...also I didn't want to get arrested again.

I'd only taken a couple of sips of the drink by the time she was stood at my side with her handbag over her shoulder, "Come on then. Where are you taking me?"

"I thought I'd treat you to a bite to eat, and I'll regale you with stories of my time spent in prison."

"Ok jailbird, sounds good to me. Just one moment." She slapped the bar with the flat of her hand and the barman turned to look at her. 'One for the road,' she shouted.

Without question, and despite the fact he was already serving someone, the barman answered the summons. He turned an empty glass in to a large vodka, added some ice, and served it to Hamster-Chick. Before the ice had chance to dilute the spirit, she drained the glass and slammed it down.

"Are you going to drink that?" she said pointing at my almost untouched pint.

"I can't drink that quickly," I said.

She picked the pint up and brought it to her lips and tipped into her mouth. I have seen kitchen sinks drain their contents slower than she emptied the glass.

When she'd finished, she grabbed my arm and marched me out of the pub.

"Where are we going then?"

"Well, do you fancy an upper class establishment or something more normal?" I asked.

"Do I look like a high class sort of girl?"

I looked her up and down. "I'll keep an eye out for a burger van."

She laughed and elbowed me in the ribs. "Cheeky. Look just something simple, pub meal will be fine by me."

"But you've been in a pub all day."

"I like pubs, that's why I work there."

"Ok, if you insist."

We walked a short distance to another gastro-pub. Except for the name, and the less attractive bar staff, it looked a lot like the pub we'd just left.

It was clear she was well known. I lost count of the amount of people she spoke to. Girls air-kissed, men hugged her. It's disturbing when other men have more physical contact with your date than you do.

"You're popular." I said.

"Perils of working in a pub, everyone knows you."

I bought a beer for me and a shot for her, before we'd even reached a table she'd relieved her glass of its contents. We'd been sat for a few minutes reading the menu when a waitress appeared. After yet another air-kiss, she took our orders.

Hamster-chick tapped her glass. "Same again," she said. The

waitress pointed at my glass with the end of her pen. I shook my head and covered the top of my drink with my hand, in case she had some special power that automatically replaced the two mouthfuls I'd already swallowed. Armed with our orders the waitress headed back to the bar. She returned a short while later with the drink, and I'm sure it didn't remain in the glass long enough to make the inside wet.

The conversation was easy. I talked about my job and she talked about raves and getting wasted. She drank steadily throughout the evening, whilst I cautiously sipped a couple of pints.

We ordered and ate food, which she washed down with several more vodkas. There are Russian sailors who don't drink as much as she did. In fact there are Russian boats that need less liquid on which to float.

It wasn't long before her eyes were unable to keep in time with the movement of her head. Each time she turned to face another direction, a second passed before the eyes caught up. The muscles in her neck worked periodically as her chin dropped towards her chest, and she had to snap it back up.

Eventually the muscles gave up altogether, her head sagged and I found myself talking to her scalp. It was the cue to go home. I'd had a few drinks and didn't want to risk driving so I pulled out my phone to call a taxi. A text message from the Receptionist was waiting to be read.

- **How's it going?**

I know it's rude to use your phone when you're out socially, especially if you're on a date, but seeing as Hamster-Chick was no longer taking an active part in the evening, I took a chance that she wouldn't mind. I typed a quick reply.

- **Don't ask.**

The reply came back almost instantaneously.

- **That bad eh? Fill me in another time. X**

I rang for a taxi which the disinterested dispatcher told me would be 15 minutes. That should be enough time to get my date outside.

I touched her arm and rubbed my hand up and down her back in an effort to wake her. I watched as a string of saliva released its grip on her bottom lip, and dropped into her lap. Her head lolled from side to side and then settled back into position.

"Hey, come on. I think it's time we got you home."

She lifted her head slowly. I only saw the whites of her eyes as she tried, but failed, to open them. Her lips parted and she attempted a smile.

"Hmmugg, dududa,ummm," she grunted.

"I'll take that as an agreement," I said.

I took her arm and pulled her to her feet. She stumbled forward against the table. I threw one of her arms across my shoulders and put my other arm around her waist. We had drawn the attention of a few of the other patrons. Some of them shook their heads and tutted. It was strange how the people who had been so eager to speak to her, were nowhere to be seen in her hour of need.

She wasn't a big girl, but a drunken, dead weight is difficult to manoeuvre. We shuffled towards the door. I pushed it open with my backside, and went outside.

She was too heavy to keep stood upright, so I seated her at one of the seats in the beer garden. I bunched up my jacket and put it on the table, then gently laid her head on top of it. I stood on the edge of the car park and waited for the taxi. I'd walked no more than six feet when I heard what sounded like the mating call of a yak, but what I knew was my date regurgitating the dinner and drinks for which I had so gallantly paid.

I turned around to see that she was in the same position. Her arms were dangling by her sides and her left cheek resting on my jacket. The only difference was the large puddle of vomit that spread across the table in front her and, of course, across my jacket. I went back and checked on her and to see if my jacket could be rescued. She wretched a couple more times. Her body convulsed, and she threw up again. She never opened her eyes.

It was time I recovered my jacket before it became beyond the healing powers of a dry-cleaner. The side of her face rested in her own vomit. Her hair was bathed in the chunky liquid, which had pooled in the folds of the garment. I grabbed the sleeve and snatched it out from under her in one quick movement, like a magician removing a tablecloth without disturbing the crockery.

As usual I acted without fully thinking through the plan. I yanked the jacket as hard as I could and it moved from underneath her, but her head snapped up and hovered for a split second about three inches above the table, before dropping back down with a thud onto the wooden surface. Not only had I tried to concuss my date, the quick flourish I'd performed with the jacket meant that I had flicked vomit all over myself.

Having been sat with her all evening, I knew what she had eaten, and I was able to match some of her earlier meal to the chunks that adorned my clothing. They were accompanied by the sweet, revolting aroma of vomit, tinged with a hint of alcohol.

I shook the coat out and did my best to get rid of as much as I could. I used my handkerchief to wipe myself down and then dropped it into an ashtray on the table. I couldn't risk accidentally blowing my nose on it later.

Car headlights swept across the car park briefly illuminating us. When it stopped I realised that it was the taxi I'd ordered. Considering Hamster Chick's state, there wasn't a driver in the world that'd be prepared to take us, but I had to chance it.

I folded and tightly rolled my jacket so that the clean part was on the outside. I then wedged it under my arm. Hamsterchick was a mess but apart from some of her hair being matted, she had escaped the worst of her own emissions simply by depositing them onto my jacket.

All I had to do was convince the driver to take us. He stayed in the car and as I walked towards him, the window slid down.

"Are you waiting for a taxi?" he asked.

"Yes," I said.

Leaning forward he peered at the alcohol casualty who was sprawled across the picnic table.

"Is she with you?" he asked nodding towards her.

I hesitated momentarily and toyed with the idea of denying any knowledge and getting into the car, after all she had left me to get arrested.

"Yes," I finally admitted.

"She doesn't look good."

Yes, thanks very much for that diagnosis doctor. "Er, no she's not, that's why I need to get her home."

"Has she puked up?"

"Yes, but I think it's out of her system now." I hoped so anyway.

"Can you assure me that she's not going to puke in my car?"

Christ what was with him? I hadn't expected to have to fill out a questionnaire before I paid for a lift home. "Well, no I can't assure that, but it's not far."

"Not sure I can take you mate, don't want a mess in my car."

"What if I hang her head out of the window? If she's sick, I'll pay for a car wash."

"Can't do it mate, contrary to health and safety," said the driver.

"What do you mean health and safety?"

"Well she might bang her head on a lamp-post or something," he said.

"Can I suggest that you don't drive too close to them then."

The driver sighed, "Look mate it's simple, your girlfriend is drunk and likely to throw up. I've got a living to earn from my car, which I can't do if it's full of puke and off the road being valeted. It's not worth my while to do that just for a few quid."

Ah, we'd arrived at the real issue, he wanted more money.

"How much?" I asked.

"Forty quid should do it."

I failed to hide my surprise. "I'm sorry, I must have missed the budget where the chancellor quadrupled taxi fares. I could hire a car for that."

"Not at this time of night you couldn't."

He was right. I knew where Hamster-chick lived, it wasn't far away and we could've probably taken a romantic stroll, if my date hadn't been unconscious. I'd had a few drinks and, even if my car hadn't been parked outside another pub, I didn't want to risk driving. The mercenary bastard was my only hope. I retrieved my wallet and handed him the cash.

"Can you give me a hand with her?" I asked.

"No chance mate, I'm not getting anything down me."

He sat in his car while I went back to Hamster-chick, hoisted her to her feet and did the shuffle again. When we reached the car the driver didn't even offer to get out and open the door. I performed a delicate balancing act, opening the door and holding her upright, whilst stopping her from planting her face into the tarmac.

I manoeuvred her into a sitting position and then sat closely beside her to prevent any slumping. Without even turning around the driver reached over the seat and pointed to a red sticker on the back of the passenger seat.

It read: 'Soiling of this vehicle will result in a £50 charge'.

Brilliant, all I had to do was stop my date from throwing up for the next few minutes.

The car set off and Hamster-chick swayed with the movement. I tried to prevent her head falling against me as her hair was still sticky and matted. The occasional moan of distress escaped her mouth as we bumped along. The stench of vomit wafted around the car, most of it probably coming from my rolled up jacket.

Having already had the fare extorted from me, I didn't have to worry about watching the meter, but I was nervous in case my date vomited again and it cost me even more. The driver seemed to be making no attempt to avoid any bumps or potholes, and he negotiated all the corners at high speed. He was trying to induce vomiting. He'd probably get his young child to clean the car, for a very small reward, and then pocket the the soiling charge. I pushed myself further against Hamster-chick and jammed her into a position where she couldn't be jostled.

The driver applied the brakes a little too sharply and jerked to a halt close to the address. I exited and rushed round to the other side to extract her before it was too late. I hauled her out of the car and propped her up again. I used my foot to push the car door shut, and before it had even closed the car was moving.

The address was a small block of flats and I had no idea which one she lived in. With the luck I was having it was guaranteed not to be situated on the ground floor, the lift wouldn't be working either.

I needed her key to open the main door to the building. I pushed her up against the wall at the side of the door, and with one hand held her in position whilst I used the other hand to search her. When I reached into the pocket of her jeans, she giggled.

"Naughty," she slurred and then slipped back into unconsciousness.

"It would be nice if you could stay conscious long enough just to get into your flat," I said pointlessly.

I pulled out a key-ring with several keys on it. Nothing indicated which one was for the door or the flat. I began the task of trying all the keys in the door, whilst ensuring my date didn't nose-dive into the concrete.

My right hand was pressed against her upper chest and neck to hold her in position whilst I stretched my left arm across to the keyhole and tried the first key. It was a struggle, and it didn't work. I made a mental note of which one I'd used, or I'd have been there all night.

I angrily muttered swear words and called my date a few choice names. As I fumbled for the next key, I saw two men walking up the path towards me. I straightened myself up.

I was stood with my hand against the throat of a unconscious young woman. It didn't look good. I moved the guilty-looking hand away so it looked less like I was strangling her. As I did she lurched forward and I instinctively put both hands out to stop her...they landed perfectly on her breasts.

Anyone seeing this would have thought that I was at best a sex-pest, and at worst a serial killer caught in the act, so they'd be forgiven if they called the police. It looked like she was going to get me arrested for a second time.

I removed my hands and I grabbed her more appropriately to stop her falling. The couple were almost upon me now, I hoped they wouldn't make some sort of citizens' arrest.

I was just about to explain myself when they skirted around me and went straight to the door. One of them looked at me and nodded, "Alright?" he said.

"Yes thanks, fine," I replied rather stupidly. Of course I wasn't fine.

The other man unlocked the door and held it wide open for me.

"Number seven." He flicked his head and looked up, indicating that the flat was indeed not on the ground floor.

"Thanks." I made my way through the doorway, it was no longer a shuffle, I had to drag her along.

"First floor, turn left," said the man who held the door.

Once I'd hauled my burden inside, they both walked away from me and stopped at a door along the corridor.

"The lift's not broken is it?" I called after them.

"No," came the reply, "there isn't one," and with that they disappeared from view, and I heard a door close.

I began my ascent to the first floor, all the time wondering how the hell murderers got rid of bodies? I know that they're not worried about injuring their victims, but it was almost impossible. I sat her down halfway up the stairs just to get my breath.

It took ten minutes to get to her front door, where I sat her on the ground and propped her back against a wall. Her head slumped forward and she was muttering incoherently to herself. I fumbled around in my pocket for the keys I'd taken off her and tried them in the lock. I missed the keyhole on my second attempt and dropped the whole bunch of keys on the floor. As I did this Hamster-Chick burst into loud, raucous laughter. I was trying to quieten her down when the door directly opposite opened and an old lady peeked around it.

"Not again," she shouted, "just get her inside and be quiet will you!" She ducked back inside and slammed the door.

I retrieved the keys and found the right one on my fourth try. The door opened onto a long hallway. The light coloured laminate floor was littered with countless shoes, each one separated from its twin by some distance. I hoisted her up to her feet, dragged her into the flat, and closed the door. I negotiated my way along the corridor, avoiding the scattered footwear.

I looked through each doorway and tried to identify a bedroom. It was the second one on the right, I think. So many clothes were strewn about that it was difficult to tell where the floor stopped and the bed began. I aimed for the highest pile of clothes, hoping it was a bed, and dropped Hamster-chick onto her back. She bounced like a rag doll and giggled quietly. The giggle turned into a cough, and she threw-up. Watery vomit spurted a short distance in the air and landed on her face and clothes. She spluttered and choked. I rolled her onto her side, she wretched, vomited again and then resumed her normal breathing.

The bed was a mess, and she was a mess. The stench was overpowering. I had planned to dump her in bed and leave, but she needed to be cleaned up. If I left she'd be discovered in a couple of days, having choked to death on her own vomit.

There was no way I could walk out on her now. I rolled her into the recovery position that I had learned years ago at school. I was thankful that she'd at least waited until she got home and hadn't done it in the taxi.

I went in search of something to clean her up. The whole house was in a similar state of disarray to the bedroom. It wasn't dirty, it was just untidy...incredibly untidy.

I found a room that was littered with hundreds of toiletries, I assumed it was the bathroom. Pants and bras hung from every makeshift hook. Towels were screwed up on the floor; I picked one up and released the aroma of fabric softener, I ran it under a tap and wet it.

I returned to the bedroom and Hamster-chick hadn't moved.

Her breathing was raspy but deep and regular. I turned her onto her back and wiped her face with the wet towel. As I did, she spat out a little more vomit.

The front of her white work shirt was stained orange and I would forever associate the tomato-based dish she'd eaten, with the smell and mess that was in front of me.

I couldn't have left her to fester in her own emissions, I had to remove her soiled clothes. I rooted through a pile of garments and found something that resembled pyjamas, they didn't match but she was in no position to object to my fashion faux pas.

Part of me had hoped that the night would end with some undressing, but I would have preferred her to be a willing participant. I approached the task in as dispassionate a way as possible. I kept my eyes on the headboard about 18 inches above her head whilst I unbuttoned her shirt. Some of the buttons were slimy and slipped through my fingers, so I had no option to look at what I was doing.

It might surprise you to know that even a man would like the first time he sees his girlfriend naked to be at least partially romantic. I imagine that it was how undertakers felt when they undress a corpse.

I removed her shirt, some of the orange stain had managed to seep through to her bra. I didn't feel right removing her underwear, so I lifted her body and pulled the pyjamas on. Then I laid her gently back down on the bed and rolled her onto her side again. I picked up the discarded dirty clothing and slid the soiled bedding out from underneath her. I looked around the flat for something that resembled a linen basket. In the end I just put the clothes on the floor in front of the washing machine, where some other dirty laundry seemed to be queued.

I stood in the doorway of the bedroom and looked at Hamster-chick. She rattled every time she exhaled. I wanted to go home, but I couldn't leave her alone. I decided to stay until she had at least emerged from the coma-like state into which she had lapsed.

I cleared a space on the floor at the side of the bed, sat down, and leaned my back against the wall. After a few minutes, I took out my phone in order to pass the time. Another text message sat there unread.

- **Is it getting any better?** It was the Receptionist.

- **It can't get any worse.**

- **Do tell.**

- **I'm in her bedroom, surrounded by discarded clothes making sure my unconscious date doesn't choke on her own vomit.**

- **You need to pick your dates more carefully. See you soon. x**

I turned my phone off and looked up at the ceiling. It was a long night.

My head jerked up, I'd nodded off and been woken by the noise of a door slamming somewhere in the flat. The bed was empty. I checked my watch, it was 6.30am. I went into the hallway and stood outside the bathroom door, I heard what I assume was a steady stream of urine trickling into a toilet bowl. Then the toilet flushed and the door opened.

The grey, make-up smudged face of Hamster Chick looked up at me, her hair looked like a few thousand volts had surged through it during the night.

"You still here?" she croaked. She brushed past my arm and returned to the bedroom, and fell onto the bed with a groan. Almost immediately she started snoring.

I retrieved my soiled coat from the floor, opened the front door, and stepped outside.

I pulled it gently closed behind me and as I turned around, the old lady from the flat opposite was stood in her doorway. It was only just getting light, what the hell was she doing up this early?

"I hope it was worth it," she said.

"Worth every penny," I replied.

- FIFTEEN -

Although she didn't know it, Hamster-chick's girlfriend audition had been a disaster. Everything was fine until she'd started drinking. I'm sure she probably didn't remember anything and she'd enjoyed herself, right up to the point where the hang-over had set in.

I decided to pick up my car and then drop into the office to collect that day's assignments before I went home to get cleaned up. I was fully aware that I smelled of the vomit with which I was splattered, but I figured that it was early Saturday morning and there'd probably be plenty of people like me doing the 'walk of shame'.

Ignoring the looks from the other customers, I grabbed a coffee from one of those generic outlets that populate most high streets.

Thankfully when I reached the newspaper office I found that it had already been unlocked. These people may have trusted me to write stories for them, but they didn't trust me with a key to their premises.

A handful of people sat at desks and tapped on computers, or murmured into phones. I picked up the small bundle of printed sheets from the tray with my name on it. A garden fete, a charity fun run, and I had to interview a family who had been made homeless by a house fire.

I leaned on the end of the desk and read the assignments. I didn't want to start or end the day on a down note, so I sandwiched the fire between the other two jobs. If I'm honest, I could never have been a big-time reporter. I don't like interviewing people who have suffered or lost something. I like happy stories, things that made me smile, or realise that there might still be some good in the world. Unfortunately nobody wants to hear good news.

"Kettle's on," a voice shouted from somewhere out of sight, it was the Receptionist.

I'd finished my bland, cardboard coffee and needed something to take the taste out of my mouth. I made my way to the small kitchen just off the main office. I found the Receptionist tending to two mugs. She stirred one, banged the teaspoon on the rim, and handed it to me.

"So, your message mentioned discarded clothes, is that in a good way?" she asked.

I sighed, "Unfortunately not. She got so drunk that she passed out. I had to take her home and put her to bed."

"Did she wake up at any stage?"

"Once I got her into her bed but only to giggle at me."

"She's won't be the first and probably not the last to laugh at you in the bedroom."

"You know how to hurt a man," I said.

"So, no sex then?"

I thought about lying but, there really was no point. "No, none at all."

"You're saying that you undressed a woman, put her to bed and got nothing for your good deeds?"

"Just lighter in the wallet from a taxi driver who doubled as a highwayman, and some slightly stained clothing."

"You do look a little," she looked me up and down, "dishevelled." She leaned forward, tugged the collar of my shirt and sniffed. "And you stink. I do hope that you're going to get washed before you actually start work."

"I was going for homeless, with a hint of wino look."

"Congratulations, you succeeded, but I reckon most people would find it unattractive."

I looked down at the dried vomit patches and the smell, that I had quite clearly gotten used to, wafted up to my nostrils. She was right, I needed to clean up.

"I can't believe that you had access to a near naked woman

and did nothing," she said.

"I never said that I hadn't done anything, I stayed up all night to make sure she didn't die a rock-star style death."

"Many a man would have taken advantage of the situation."

"I've been arrested for being drunk already this week, I can't afford to add a charge of sexual assault to my criminal record."

"You might be a drug-taking, drunken liar, with a knack for getting into the most incredible situations, but you're actually not a bad person are you?' She pinched my right cheek between her thumb and forefinger.

The coffee was scalding hot, but I took a couple of long swigs, just because I didn't know what to say next.

Lost for words, I patted her on the shoulder, like she was one of my male friends. "Thanks for the pep talk, I'll see you later."

"Keep me updated on the next date," she called after me, as I walked out of the kitchen.

I'd finished the interview with the family and returned to the blackened scar that was once their home. Macro Mike wanted a few provocative pictures; scorched photographs, charred teddy bears, that sort of thing. It felt wrong, as if I was a trespasser stood on the grave of the family's memories.

During the interview the parents recalled the events of the fire and it brought them to tears, their whole life had gone. Luckily the children were too young to fully understand, but they still wondered where their toys were.

Even the suggestion that there'd been people in similar situations who hadn't been so lucky offered no consolation. Other people's problems don't make your's any less significant.

After the flames have been extinguished and the smoke drifted, the smell of a fire sticks to clothing. I had a new scent on my clean clothes, the aroma of despair and a life-time of lost memories. Only the memories themselves weren't lost, it was just the physical representations. Photographs, mementoes, souvenirs all gone.

The family went back to their temporary accommodation

and, as I surveyed the crater I wondered what sort of God would allow this to happen to a hard-working family. I suppose that the pro-deity lobby would suggest that incidents like this were sent to test a person's resolve. If he wanted to do that why couldn't there be a written test? They're less dangerous and don't involve any mental scarring. These profound thoughts rampaged through my head when the phone in my pocket vibrated with a text message.

- Are you free tomorrow morning?

It was God-groupie. My thoughts had obviously angered some omnipresent being, who had activated one of its followers with orders to bring the blasphemer into line.

I usually spent Sundays in bed since I'd given up trawling parks for local football matches on which to report. There was a myriad of would-be journalists who liked to report on their own child's team. There was also the issue of explaining to parents why a lone male, without any children, was watching an under 12s match. When challenged I'd tell them I was a talent scout, but that encouraged too many football related questions that I couldn't answer, so I stopped going altogether.

I was apprehensive, I'd fallen for the 'Sunday dinner' trick last time, and couldn't cope with further embarrassment at the hands of her family. I didn't fancy subjecting myself to a rematch. I didn't want to spend the day re-living the humiliation where I'd spent the dinner from hell, with the family from heaven. I must've spent too long deliberating as the phone rang.

"Hi," she said, "I wasn't sure you'd got my text. Are you ok?"

A phone call immediately after a text was another tick in the 'bit too keen' box, but there was genuine concern in her voice.

"Sorry, I'm working. I'm at a house destroyed by fire and I really couldn't talk."

There was an audible almost theatrical gasp, "Oh no, that's terrible. Is everyone ok? Nobody died did they?"

"Everyone is fine."

"Was it a family?"

"Yes, parents and two young children."

"Oh no. I'll say a prayer for them as soon as I get off the phone."

As I looked across at the charcoal remains of the family's life I felt a little angry. It wasn't prayers they needed to bring back all their worldly possessions, it was a time machine. Leave religion out of it, and the reparation to the insurance company.

"I am free tomorrow, but I'm not so sure that your family will want to see me again. I don't think I made a good impression the first time around," I said.

"Oh, don't worry about them. They're very forgiving."

Christians seem to do that a lot, but I guess if the figure-head of your religion can forgive the people who nailed him to a cross, then his followers can forgive someone for frisbee-ing a prophylactic across their dinner table.

"I'm still feeling embarrassed. Being stuck in a room with them might be a bit intense. Can we go somewhere else? You know with a some other people around."

"I understand completely. Look, just come here for about 10 o'clock and we'll take it from there."

"Dinner out?" I asked.

"I think we could do that."

"Without the family?" I said tentatively.

"Whatever makes you feel comfortable. You'll need to see them, I think it'd be rude otherwise."

She was right, her father would have another reason to hate me if I just turned up and whisked his daughter away for dinner without saying anything.

"Ok, I'll see you tomorrow."

"Good. Looking forward to it. Bye and God bless."

"Bye."

So, I had to meet the family again, but I would try to make any interaction as short as humanly possible.

My last assignment took a little longer than expected. I called the newspaper office and I spoke to the Receptionist to ask if she'd keep the office open, so that I could type and submit my stories before the end of the day. When I walked through the door, she was sat with her feet on a desk, her thumbs moving in a blur over the screen of her mobile phone.

"You took your time," she said without looking up.

"Either you want the job done quick or you want it done properly," I replied, "if I do something, I do it properly."

"Does the same go for your relationships?"

"Yes, that's why I didn't jump for the first girl that came my way."

"And why you're auditioning three for your Ex-Factor," she said, placing her phone on the desk.

"I'll admit, I've got myself into a situation but I'm working it out. I think I'm down to two now."

"You are?" she said surprised. "Who's been voted out?"

"The party animal."

"Why?"

"It's not going to work out. Her life-style is a little too hectic for my liking. The only thing we have in common, is the inability to remain conscious during a date."

"Anything else to tell?" she asked.

"I have another second date tomorrow."

"Which one this time?"

"The religious one."

She let out a giggle. "Ah, the condom throwing incident."

"Yes, but thankfully she's promised I won't be spending lunch with the family."

Her phone made a brief drill noise as it vibrated against the desktop, indicating another incoming text. She reached for the phone, flipped it over and began the manual dexterity exercises that went with typing.

Almost without a break in the conversation she continued talking. "So you probably won't see Granny's fanny then?"

"I hope not."

I marvelled at the way she could simultaneously continue a verbal conversation with one person, and a text conversation with another. True evidence of a woman's ability to multi-task.

"What's the plan then?" she asked, as her thumbs whizzed

over the screen of her phone.

"I'm going to pick her up and then we'll go for an early dinner."

"Together? Alone?"

"I made sure of it."

She put the phone down again. "You'll have to let me know how it goes."

She got up from the chair and headed towards the kitchen. "I'll make a drink but don't be long. I've stayed on to keep the office open just for you. I can't be late, I've got a date tonight."

"Really." It came out a bit more incredulous than I'd intended.

"Don't sound so surprised, believe it or not you don't have the monopoly on relationships," she laughed. "Monopoly. That means just one doesn't it? I guess that's not the right word where you're concerned."

"Who is he? Do I know him?" I asked.

She stopped in the doorway to the kitchen area and turned to face me.

"Two things; firstly I don't have to answer your questions seeing as you're not my mum, and secondly, who said anything about it being a man!" She winked and disappeared through the door.

My heart skipped slightly and I forced my brain to ignore the images it had decided to form. I tried to continue the conversation.

"Er, I hope it goes ok." Were the only words I managed to say.

I switched the computer on and concentrated on preparing the article, but I have to admit I was struggling to think straight.

Within a few minutes a cup of coffee was put down in front of me. The Receptionist leaned over me and spoke softly in my ear, "I'll leave you to your thoughts, whatever they maybe, but like I said don't be too long. One of us might be getting sex tonight."

She sat at another desk studying her phone. She didn't speak again. It took much longer than it should have done to complete the article, because my mind wasn't on the task.

When I finally submitted my writing with the press of a button, the Receptionist sensed I had finished and stood up. She pushed her phone into the front pocket of her tight jeans.

"Come on stud," she ruffled my hair, "if you're lucky, next time we meet I'll give you all the sordid details of my date."

I followed her out of the office and onto the street. She locked the door, pocketed the key and then kissed me on the cheek. "Wish me luck, and don't forget, let me know how it goes." With that she turned and walked up the street.

My brain had fuzzed over slightly, "Yeah, okay. Enjoy your date," I called after her.

- SIXTEEN -

I didn't take the liberty of parking on the drive of the big house; I didn't want to reignite the fire of hatred that I'd lit under father, before I'd even knocked on the door. As I crunched along the gravel, the front door opened and the family surged out.

"Hello doctor," said Granny, but before she could say anything else, or show me an intimate body part, the family ushered her away like celebrity bodyguards. Only father remained in the open doorway.

He didn't speak to me, he regarded me in much the same way people do when they find skid marks in public toilets. He shouted back into the house, "He's here," and with that he joined the rest of the family in the people carrier, the one with a rudimentary drawing of a fish on the tailgate. I watched as they drove away.

It was the perfect interaction, short and sweet…ok, maybe not sweet.

When I turned around, my date was stood in the doorway.

"Family outing?" I asked.

"Sundays are for family." She leaned forward and kissed me on the cheek.

She grabbed a handbag from the hallway floor, stepped outside, and locked the door behind her.

"Where are we going?" I asked.

"Let's get into the car, and I'll direct you."

In-between directions there was small talk. I'd missed breakfast so I was hungry and although I'd never used the word brunch, I was definitely ready to embrace the concept.

"Just round the next corner," she said, and then pointed to the left. "Park here."

I looked around, there was no restaurant nearby, no pub, or even a cafe shed. There was however, a church.

She jumped out of the car, and I warily followed. I had a feeling in the pit of my stomach that I probably wouldn't get to experience brunch after all. I joined her on the pavement, she took my hand and led me away from the car, in the direction I definitely didn't want to go. When I say that she led the way, it was more like I was being dragged.

There's a scene in the film 'The Omen', where the child of the devil goes berserk when he is taken to a church by his adoptive parents. At that moment I contemplated imitating the child and flipping my lid, but I figured that it'd do nothing for the continuation of any potential relationship.

I paused momentarily as I stepped through the doorway, waiting for the crash of thunder and the flash of lightning, as God smited the blasphemer. I don't know what it takes for the almighty to put you on the train to hell, but I'm pretty sure drinking, drug-taking, and dating three women at the same time, would qualify me for a first class ticket on the Satan Express. When there was no flash or crash, I followed my date into the dimly lit cave. I'm sure the beginning of the bible mentions something about 'Let there be light', and it's unfortunate that the church-goers don't take it literally and add a couple of bulbs here and there just to brighten things up.

Churches are cold, that is unless you find a seat next to the single small, Victorian radiator that's fighting hard to provide the congregation with some of the warmth of God.

I know it sounds like I'm anti-religion, but I've had some bad experiences in churches. When I was younger my parents made me go to Sunday School. They weren't religious themselves but they wanted me to have some sort of moral guidance that they couldn't provide. Considering the fact I had become a womanising drunk, with a sideline in drug abuse, I figured it hadn't worked.

Every Sunday morning Dad took me to church, left me at the door and then disappeared for a 'walk'. I suspect that this 'walk' took him past a pub, as he smelled of cigarettes and beer by the time he picked me up.

Sunday School was horrible, it was almost the same as school, but with only one subject. The teachers were always ancient and were never happy when you asked difficult questions like, 'Did Noah house the tigers with the antelope?', and "Why did Adam and Eve have belly buttons?"

Soon after I joined Sunday School I was targeted by bullies. It culminated in the red pencil I was using to colour my drawing of the crucifixion, being snatched by a bully who used it to stab me in the leg. Things went downhill after that.

If God failed to protect me in his own house, what chance did I stand in the outside world? I never told my parents, so I had to find a way to convince them not to take me any more. Dad took a lot more convincing than Mum, after all his Sunday 'walk' was at stake. It was only when, at the age of 9, I learned the word 'atheist' that Mum decided to pull the plug on my morality training.

Shortly afterwards we got a family dog that needed a walk at the same time every Sunday morning.

By entering the church we had lowered the average age of the congregation by about 25 years. We slipped into one of the pews, that were so highly polished pews I did actually slip. I couldn't lean back because this just made my backside slide off, so I sat, uncomfortably, bolt upright. I had just thought that things couldn't get any worse when my date was tapped on the shoulder. We both turned around. It was her father, flanked by the rest of the family. Sat right at the very end of their pew was Granny, who I swear gave me a cheeky, little wink.

Father's face lit up when he saw his daughter but any light was immediately extinguished when he looked at me sat beside her. I turned to face the front, but I could feel his eyes as they bored into the back of my head.

God-groupie passed me a hymn book, grabbed my hand and held it tight. I think she was worried in case I made a break for the exit. The vicar/bishop, or whatever he was, stepped out from behind a curtain and climbed into the pulpit. He raised his hymn book and I examined the front of my copy. I hadn't realised that everybody had stood up, and I'd remained seated, for what could have only been a few seconds. A sigh of disgust was exhaled somewhere behind me. Cut me some slack will you, I'm new to this cult thing.

An organ started playing from an unseen location in the building, and people had already started singing. I was still staring at the bland cover of my hymn book.

God-groupie used her own open book and pointed towards a wooden board on the wall to the side of the pulpit. It had tiles with numbers written on them slotted into grooves, they were hymn numbers. For heaven's sake! Why, in the 21st Century, wasn't it computerised? They could have slide-show presentations with bullet points for the ten commandments, and online polls where you could vote for your favourite disciple.

Due to the fact that my date had intertwined her fingers with mine, I only had the use of one hand, which I used to flick the pages of my hymn book, trying to match the number on the board to one in my book. I used my thumb to find a page and then held it open with my chin. God-groupie released my trapped hand and took the book off me. She deftly found the page I needed, handed the book back and grabbed my hand again. She did all this while still singing the hymn. Damn she knew the words!

As every neighbour I've ever had will testify, I cannot sing. I don't pretend to be able to do so either. I do it on my own, in the privacy of my own house, and nowhere else. At this point I was expected to sing in public, along with a group of elderly backing singers.

Hymns are like some sort of karaoke nightmare. I had a set lyrics in front of me, and I had to make them fit to a tune that I'd never heard before. There had to be a knack to it though, everyone else seemed to be doing fine. Words like 'almighty' and '*glory*' were repeated frequently, and there were choruses, why are there always choruses? It just drags the song out and prolongs the agony. My schooldays meant that I knew the words to one hymn, 'Morning has broken', but if I'm honest I probably actually only knew the first verse.

I went through the motions and mimed. Directly behind me, her father belted out the words with such passion that I felt spittle hit the back of my neck, it burned like little drops of acid. I'm sure he was doing it on purpose.

Everyone was lost in their own Christian sing-a-long. There were about twenty different voices and if I listened carefully I could hear every single one, from the croaky old lady on the front row, to the quiet singing of the woman who had a vice-like grip on my right hand.

After what seemed like an eternity, the song ended. The echoes of the last words hadn't even died down, when everyone sat down and the rabbi/iman started his sermon. I had no idea what he was talking about, but I know it was dull, extremely dull.

To make matters worse my phone vibrated in my pocket as a message landed. I'd remembered to turn it to silent, but surrounded by these ancient walls it sounded like a woodpecker hammering on the wooden pew. It would have alleviated some of the boredom, but I thought it would be bad form to retrieve it and read the text. Although I was pretty sure that it wouldn't have made things much worse.

My eyes felt irritated and the lids became extremely heavy. My mind was wandering and the words I could hear being spoken were swimming around my head, making less sense than they had been previously. My head sagged forward and my chin bounced off my chest, accompanied by a snort. Okay, not a snort, a snore. I had no idea how long I'd been asleep. I glanced around and a few people were looking in my direction. Damn! It had not gone unnoticed. My date stared straight ahead, in what was an obvious attempt not to draw attention to me. The heads of my detractors snapped forward as the Arch Bishop/Pope neared the end of his sermon, and they all muttered a dreary 'amen'.

One person was definitely still looking at me; I could feel the heat as his stare lasered through my spinal stem.

I blinked a few times and rubbed my thighs with the one hand that was free, and prepared to leave. I hadn't listened to anything that was being said and when everyone stood up, I was ready to depart, but my heart sank when everybody else lifted their hymn books and readied themselves. The mysterious organist began playing again, and everyone started singing yet another unidentifiable song. Oh God, how long could it possibly go on? I'd been there for a full 15 minutes already.

I resigned myself to standing there with my mouth clamped shut whilst everyone else praised the lord through the power of song.

When they'd finished, it suddenly became interactive. Everyone turned to the person next to them, held hands tenderly, and simultaneously said, "Peace and love be with you." They then hugged each other.

God-groupie, pulled the hand that she was still clutching and turned me to face her. She grabbed my other hand in the same grip and stared at me. She squeezed gently and softly said, "Let peace and love be with you." I had never before heard someone say anything with such feeling and meaning. I was so taken aback that I forgot that I should have probably said the same.

I muttered something, but never actually formed the words. She pulled me towards her, released my hand, and threw both arms around me, and squeezed me tightly. I gingerly put my hand on her back, and we lingered momentarily. I tried to ignore the fact that I could feel her breasts as they pressed into my chest. I let go and moved back a little bit quicker than was probably necessary, because her father's stare was now getting to work on the side of my head.

As I let her go, she turned to the person next to her and repeated the greeting. At that point I was glad that I'd sat at the end of a row as there was no-one next to me with which to make this creepy, uncomfortable exchange. The church was filled with a low murmur as everyone uttered the same words.

I stood still and waited for them to finish, when someone tapped me on the shoulder. I instinctively turned and father looked straight at me with a humourless smile on his face. I thought I'd made some error that even a Christian would be unable to forgive. I looked around from some sort of guidance. I saw that everyone was making this gesture to the people on the four compass points around them. Father held out his hand. I refused to show any weakness so thrust my own out to meet it. It was enveloped in a tight, clammy grip. He applied more pressure than a Christian probably should, constricting the bones in my hand.

He curled back his lips to reveal two rows of teeth, that looked like a untended headstones in a cemetery, at midnight. I realised that I hadn't seen him smile last time we met, but then again I hadn't given him anything to be happy about.

His teeth stayed together as he said, "Peace and love be with you". He yanked my arm towards him as he went in for the hug. The movement was so sudden that I got knocked off balance and considered contacting an injury lawyer about a whiplash claim. I almost fell across the back of the pew. He released my hand, and both his arms snaked around me as he brought me into a crushing embrace. He slowly increased the pressure, in much the same way as an anaconda, and placed his head over my left shoulder.

I felt his warm breath as he hissed quietly into my ear, "Step out of line and I'll break your legs." If I'd thought his daughter had spoken the sincerest words I'd ever heard, then I'd been mistaken.

He uncoiled his arms, setting me free. I straightened up and looked around. No-one else had heard it. I faced him as he stared straight through me, his face expressionless.

I was reluctant to turn my back on the man who had quietly threatened to cripple me, but I eventually faced the front. My date grabbed my hand again and I risked a glance over my shoulder. He didn't even look in my direction.

The service was on a loop. There was a sermon then a hymn,

then a sermon again. These were punctuated by the odd, 'amen' or, 'praise the lord'.

I was paying very little attention as I was reconsidering my opinion of Christians. I had always thought that they were gentle, loving, accepting, and forgiving. My opinion had changed in a matter of moments. His words had been as menacing as his daughter's had loving. It wasn't a threat, it was a promise. Okay, so it had been conditional, "If you step out of line," he had said, but let's be honest I'd been such an idiot, that I wasn't even sure where that line was.

Everybody had their hands clasped and heads bowed. The recitation of the lord's prayer was bringing the whole thing to an end. I knew I had just met real evil, and I needed someone to deliver me from it.

We shuffled out of the pews and into the aisle. Everyone was moving slowly and I wondered what was causing the hold up. As we reached the door, I discovered the reason for the traffic jam. Everyone was filing past the high-priest/reverend in single file. I'm not sure how he arrived there before everyone else, but churches probably had hidden doors and secret passageways.

He shook the hand of everyone and exchanged a few words before he released them. As I arrived in front of him I offered my hand and he took it in his soft, squidgy palm and placed his other hand over the top.

"And who's this?" he asked.

"A friend of mine," God-groupie answered.

"Ah, a new member of the family," he said, "I do hope you enjoyed the service."

I nodded and managed a 'Yes,' I still didn't know how to address him and wasn't even sure whether I should bow.

"I think you'll like it here. We're like one big family. We share our troubles, and take care of each other's problems."

I couldn't be sure, but I thought his eyes flicked towards her father before they landed back on me. Was this some sort of mafia family that I'd stumbled into? If he had tried to pull me in for an embrace I'd have been a little concerned, but if he had gone for the full-on kiss on the lips, I'd actively resist; I'd seen 'The Godfather'.

I extracted myself from his doughy grasp, leaving his hand floating where I'd left it. It was adorned in a some sort of religious jewellery. If he expected me to kiss his ring, he could kiss mine!

'Nice' is such a horrible word, it's so non-descriptive and lacks the impact of more expressive words. I've never liked it and I try not to use it, but I have to say that when we were left on our own, we found a pub and I had a 'nice' time.

She was pleasant and good company. The best thing about the date was that I didn't have to remember what lies I'd told her. I ate what I wanted, and I could be my own age. I told her all about myself, within reason of course, there were some things, especially about my recent past, that I couldn't share with her, as they would have clashed with her beliefs.

She enjoyed a couple of glasses of wine and I stuck to the soft drinks. I was glad to see that she drank alcohol, but not to excess. The conversation covered my job, her hobbies, a little bit of politics, and some holiday stories...but not all.

Throughout the date I couldn't shake the echoes of the whisper in my ear, and what amounted to a promise to cause me serious injury. I wondered exactly what I could do that would over-step the line. I'm pretty sure that if I actually slept with his daughter, I wouldn't have just stepped over the line, I'd have vaulted it.

She chatted away and I made a couple of noises just so she knew that I was listening, but in reality my brain had wandered elsewhere and I was visualising myself sat in a wheelchair, whilst I ate my food through a straw. I know he hadn't mentioned that last bit but my imagination was running wild.

My arms were too weak to propel me in a wheelchair, which would mean I'd need one of those motorised versions. This would mean less exercise and consequential weight gain. I'd end up grossly obese and unable to move. I'd be confined to my bedroom with an army of carers who'd find large bits of uneaten food in the folds of my skin. My stomach stapling surgery would be the subject of a documentary which would only be released after my early death.

My phone vibrated twice in my pocket, so imperceptible that it could've been mistaken for a muscle twitch. Fishing it out would be rude, but right at that moment I wanted to read that text, which told me I wasn't really interested in the conversation.

She continued chatting and I added the odd understanding nod. A couple more minutes passed and the phone repeated its buzz, it felt more insistent this time as though it knew it was being ignored. I still didn't look at it, I'd probably wait until she visited the toilet.

God-groupie talked and I pretended to listen, but I had lost myself in the mystery that surrounded the sender of my message. There weren't many people who would know I was on a date, so whoever it was probably had no idea that they were interrupting the courtship ritual of the lesser-spotted, lying journalist.

It wasn't Bestie, he never sent messages, he aways called. He claimed I was more likely to pick the phone up if he rang rather than answer a text message, which was true. It wouldn't be Mum, she hadn't quite got used to texting, she usually did it without her glasses on and they came across as though they were written in Welsh. Dad hadn't even grasped the concept of sending a message, he was still trying to come to terms with the decline of the telegram.

I mentally checked off names in my head until I decided that it was probably the Receptionist; it'd be another job. Then I realised that it was Sunday and she shouldn't be at work. That never stopped her sending a text before. The more I thought about it, the more it seemed likely that it was her, after all she'd sent messages before when I was out with a woman.

I realised I had been inert for a few minutes so I nodded a couple of times just to let God-groupie know I hadn't died, or slipped into a coma. Then I realised it had gone quiet. I honed back in on the moment.

She raised her eyebrows and tilted her head slightly. Oh God, she'd asked a question, and I'd missed it. I'd been so engrossed in the identity of the mystery sender of the text message, that I'd paid absolutely no attention to what was being said just two feet in front of me.

There was no telling how long she'd been waiting for an answer? It didn't matter, I knew I had been silent for longer than was comfortable.

"So, what do you think?" she asked.

Oh no, she'd asked for an opinion. I couldn't just blag this with a simple yes or no, it required a more thorough reply.

"I don't know, it depends," I said vaguely.

"On what?"

"A number of factors," I said. I'd done it again, why couldn't I admit that I'd not listened to her. I could say I'd lost myself looking into her eyes, or that I was thinking about how beautiful she was. There were a myriad of excuses available.

"I know it's difficult, you've not known me that long, but I promise you I won't judge you on your answer."

For God's sake! It wasn't just a straight-forward question either. I don't care what she'd just said, she would judge me on whatever came out of my mouth next. My mind raced. The phone vibrated again.

You can butt out, you caused all this. I screamed to myself.

I tried to look like I was giving my answer some serious thought. "I know you said you won't judge me, but the fact that you're saying that makes me worry that you might."

She reached across the table and grabbed my hand. "I swear I won't judge you, I'm the one that asked. There's no pressure."

I attempted an expression that would convey some sort of internal turmoil, in the hope that she repeated the question, but in truth I probably just looked like I was constipated.

She squeezed my hand. "Look, we've had a couple of dates, you've met my family. It seems like the next logical step."

My change of expression was immediate, from constipation

to shock. Whoa, had she proposed? Two dates, met the family, next logical step? She'd counted the meal as a date. I'd met her family, we'd then gone to church, and now she wanted to get married.

"Don't you think it's a bit quick?" I asked.

"I'm not usually this forward but this just feels right. We get on really well and I thought you felt the same, I feel a bit silly now. I've misinterpreted everything." She sounded disappointed.

I took a long look at her. I could only describe her as beautiful. She was kind, gentle, but a little too forward. She had a great smile, and I was clearly more important to her than I'd previously thought. Any man would be proud to have her as his wife, but I couldn't rush into it. I'd heard of whirlwind romances, but I was in the middle of a full blown tornado.

I put my other hand on top of hers. "It's not your fault," I said, "I'm just not ready for that kind of commitment. It may seem right, but we've not known each other for five minutes. I'm a big believer in getting to know someone first."

She nodded and smiled a sad smile. "You're right, I'm sorry. I should never have asked. It's just the family will be away later this week, and I thought we could do it while the house is empty."

Now the confusion set in. She wanted to get married while the family were away? That made no sense, and why did she need the house to be empty?

She leaned forwarded across the table and closed the gap between us. She lowered her voice, "It's just that a couple of dates kind of makes us boyfriend and girlfriend and I thought that making love to you would cement our relationship and show my commitment."

What!

No, no, no!

It wasn't marriage she'd suggested, it was sex. She'd asked if I wanted to sleep with her, and I hadn't been listening. Damn you phone, I'm finding another sea to throw you into. I'd just said that I wouldn't have sex with someone until I knew them better, I couldn't recover from that.

No. no. no!

What the hell had I done? I'd been offered sex on a plate and I'd turned it down. I wasn't actually turning down the sex, I was turning down the marriage proposal that was never actually made.

No, no, no!

She brought her other hand up and rested it on top of mine. My brain suddenly shouted, "One potato, two potato…" for no apparent reason, but then it had just had a shock and wasn't acting rationally. She patted my hand and lowered her voice even further. "I wanted it to be special, you know, my first time."

No, no, no!

I went home and cried myself to sleep.

- SEVENTEEN -

Despite my Sherlock Holmes-style deductions, the text message that had started the problem had been from some cold calling company asking whether I'd ever had PPI. I remembered the company name with the intention of unleashing the anger of my pent up sexual frustration on them the next time they called.

In truth, I knew it wasn't their fault. I hadn't listened to my date. I should've given her my undivided attention, but I was more concerned with the possibility of a message from the woman who allocated my work. Which was why I made an unannounced trip to the office that morning.

She was sat in her normal chair. The Receptionist, the office dogsbody, but looking for all the world like the managing director. She saw me as I pushed open the door and raised her coffee mug in my direction. "Your round, lover-boy," she shouted.

I grabbed her mug out of her hand as I walked past and went straight to the kitchen. I was filling the kettle, as she walked in behind me.

The tap choked and then spat out water with all the ferociousness of a geyser unleashing itself after a thousand years of pressure build up. After yesterday, I knew how it felt. The water splashed the front of my trousers. I hadn't realised how light-coloured they were until the water darkened them.

I filled the kettle and switched it on, it growled quietly as it warmed up. A small, attention-attracting cough made me turn around, and the Receptionist was leaning on the jamb in the open doorway, with her arms folded.

She raised her eyebrows and nodded towards my groin. "I take it you're excited to see me," she said.

I brushed myself down and tried to get rid of the excess water. "No, it's the tap."

"Would you like me to help you brush it off?"

A sudden inexplicable jolt of electricity shot through my abdomen, like a bolt of lightning looking for a somewhere to earth itself. My cheeks tinged and I blushed. I turned back around and rearranged a couple of mugs for no reason other than to hide my reaction.

"Er, no I meant the water was a bit fast, the tap is a little bit too eager to please."

"It's not the only one," she smiled.

I felt warm and at a loss for words. I needed something to moisten, my previously unnoticed, dry mouth. A change of subject was required.

"So what have you got for me today?" I asked.

"Not so fast, oh great spinner of romantic lies and snarer of vulnerable women. You owe me an update on your latest conquest." She walked into the room, pulled out one of the dining chairs and sat down. She put her elbows on the Swedish, formerly flat-packed table and rested her chin in both palms. The kettle rattled on its base as the contents boiled.

I leaned back on the kitchen work-top and regained some of my composure. "I'm not sure where to start."

"Start at the very beginning, that's a very good place to start."

"We're quoting the Sound of Music are we? Funny, but I never had you down as a nun," I joked.

"Well spotted, ten points to the journalist, but five points deducted for trying to avoid the question."

"Seriously, I have no idea where to begin."

Behind me the kettle clicked off, I poured the contents into the mugs and prepared two steaming hot coffees while the conversation continued.

"Well," she said, "was it good or bad?"

"I'd have to say bad."

"Which part was bad?" she asked.

"Well, the date began with a church service, then her father threatened to maim me. I was then introduced to the head of some mafia family who was trying to pass himself off as a man of God. I spent the rest of the date fearing for my knee-caps."

I picked up the two mugs, I placed one on the table in front of her and kept the other to myself.

"That's definitely not good, but I've heard of worse dates, in fact I've been on worse dates."

"That's the 'not so good' bit," I said, "I haven't even got to the bad bit yet."

"How could it get any worse?" she said.

"Well, we then went for dinner," I pre-empted the question she was about to ask, "just the two of us. It was okay, but at some stage I stopped listening to her talking and just switched off, which is when I missed it."

"Missed what?"

"The part where she offered me sex."

Her head shot up from where it rested on her hands. "What?"

"She said she wanted to sleep with me."

"Wow, that escalated quickly. From not so good to awesome, in a very short space of time."

"Not really, I said it went from bad to worse."

"How can it get worse? A woman has just offered to get jiggy with you."

"Well, I wasn't listening so I thought she was proposing, and I turned her down."

There was a split second where the interested look on her face froze. A crease of confusion appeared on her forehead, and then disappeared as she realised what I had said. She collapsed into fits of laughter. She didn't speak for a long time.

Eventually, through gasps of breath, she said, "You were offered sex on a plate, and you turned it down because you thought it was a marriage proposal. That is the funniest thing I have ever heard."

"It isn't funny. She was the last one of the three that I thought would ever offer me sex. I can't say I hadn't entertained the idea, but I never thought there'd be any chance, then out of the blue, she comes out with that."

The Receptionist gently dabbed the corners of her eyes, and wiped away the tears without smudging her make-up.

"So what are you going to do now?"

"I'm going to have to call it off. I made it clear that it was too early to make a commitment. Now she thinks I'm some sort of celibate angel, that won't sleep with someone until I know them better. And when I say know someone better, to her that'll mean marriage."

The Receptionist bit her bottom lip while she tried to stop herself laughing any further, "But what if she is 'the one', you know the girl you are meant to spend the rest of your life with?"

"She isn't, I can't see myself spending my life with that girl. She's beautiful, she has an incredible body, but she's nice. I don't think I want nice. The fact that I wasn't listening to her yesterday tells me that I'm not interested in what she's got to say."

"Perhaps you were slightly preoccupied with the death threats from Daddy to concentrate. If you were to make an honest woman of her than he might start to like you."

She was right, I had been more concerned with the threats than the conversation, but if I really had liked her, then that wouldn't have mattered. "I don't know, I just don't think it's right at all."

"She is the only one you haven't lied to, that's got to count for something."

I shrugged.

"So what do you want, if you don't want 'nice'?" she asked.

"I don't know. I need a bit of abuse every now and again. I don't want someone to agree with everything I say. I don't want someone to take me too seriously. I just know I don't want 'nice'."

"You could be in a for a long wait then."

"So how did your date go?" I asked.

"Well, let's just say I didn't miss the hint."

"What? Damn it. Well at least one of us had sex last night."

She nodded and immediately glazed over. She stared at some object in the distance, probably reliving the events of the previous evening.

"Is he potential boyfriend material? You can tell me about your sexual experience and how he was, if you want." It was my turn to smile.

"Firstly I already told you, I'd never said it was a man and secondly, I never said there was just one of them."

She stood up, picked up her coffee mug, and left the room.

I was still reeling from the images that had been planted in my head long after I had collected my jobs and left the building. They niggled me for the next few hours and did nothing to help my sexual frustration. I floated through the day, failing to concentrate on the tasks in hand.

When my mobile phone trilled sharply, I couldn't rescue it from my pocket quick enough. I don't know what I was expecting, but it wasn't a message from Right-on.

- Do you fancy meeting up?

I hadn't spoken to her since she'd served me the inedible meal, and I'd ran out on her after she'd inflicted the third degree burns. I'd resigned myself to the fact that I probably wouldn't hear from her again. So I was slightly elated that she had bothered to get back in contact.

She was also the only candidate left. I was pretty sure that I wouldn't hear from Hamster Chick again, she was probably continuing to stumble from bed to drink and back again, without another thought for me. There was the outside chance that she might have felt embarrassed about the whole incident, but I doubted it.

It's possible that God-groupie would be put off by, what she thought, was my take on sex before marriage, but was actually my stance on marriage before a third date! It might not be the right thing to say, but I believe that sex before marriage is vital. It's the only way you'll know if you are compatible on all levels.

Maybe I could go back on my mistaken morality and persuade her that, after a lot of soul searching, I had decided that sleeping together wasn't such a bad idea. Why not add hypocrisy to my growing list of vices? She was more eager about our relationship than I was; I couldn't keep leading her on because I knew deep down that she wasn't the one.

Right-on had been the unattainable woman of my adolescent years, and the only one to have made it through the auditions. I needed to give her another chance, perhaps everything would 'click' this time. I convinced myself that if I ignored her personal traits, then it would work. I couldn't come clean about my non-vegetarianism, not just yet. Then she'd know I was lying. At some stage in our future, I'd come up with an elaborate plan to introduce meat into my diet. Maybe I'd feign some illness that required a daily intake of steak to prevent my death. I'd work something out.

I replied to her message, and agreed to meet in a pub that evening. If she thought my choice of venue was a bit out of town, she never mentioned it, but I had to pick a pub that I'd not been to with either of the other two women.

The date was arranged, and at least I had something to divert my mind away from its current obsession with the Receptionist's love-life.

- EIGHTEEN -

My taxi arrived early and I scoped out the location, to ensure that it wasn't hosting some sort of Christian beer festival, or that Hamster-chick wasn't taking part in an out-of-town pub crawl.

It was an old style pub so wasn't filled with office-dwellers who had stopped for a bite to eat and a quick pint on their way home to their yuppie lifestyles. It was the natural habitat of the local, the only office that some of these people had seen, was a benefit office. They swallowed the hard-earned gains of the tax payers' contributions like vampires let loose in a blood bank.

The low muttering of voices was punctuated by the soft thunk of a dart hitting a board, and the skittering of dominoes as they were shuffled around a table.

Despite the ban, I smelled cigarette smoke, not the old, stale smell, but fresh-out-of-the-lungs smoke. This was a pub stuck in time.

As I approached the bar, I realised that my plan to order a half pint of lager would probably result in me being beaten to death for ordering a 'girl's drink'. A place like this probably didn't even stock half pint glasses. After making a show of scrutinising the hand pumps, I ordered a pint of real ale.

A few of the regulars raised their personally engraved tankards to their lips, glancing sideways at me as they drank. I gave a weak smile and tried not to draw too much attention to the fact I was an interloper.

The grizzled barman poured the pint. It slopped around in the glass, the frothy head spilling over the sides and down onto his hand, he then plonked it down in front of me. I gave him a note in payment and he scratched around in the drawer of an old cash register before returning my change. I held out my hand and the money fell into my palm, along with the froth that the pint glass had been unable to hold.

I stuffed the wet coins into my pocket. I dried my hand on the outside of my trousers, as I nursed my over-full drink of 'Ferret's Greasy Nipple' towards an empty table in the corner. There were two chairs and an apparently unread, copy of yesterday's newspaper rested next to a small glass vase with a single flower in it. It was obviously unoccupied. If I sat with my back to the wall, it would allow a good view of the door so I could see my date arrive, and it also meant that I could keep an eye on the other customers.

As I moved into position and my backside hovered over the chair, it was as if I had flicked some sort of 'off' switch. The barman stopped dead, the tea-towel that would have been of interest to the Environmental Health department, froze inside the glass he was drying. The shuffling of dominoes ceased. Even the jukebox switched off, or at least I think it did, I'm not even sure that it was playing in the first place. I could have sworn that a single dart stopped in mid air about two feet from its target. If there'd been a whippet under a chair, it would have looked up at me.

A sea of faces were turned in my direction and, although I knew there was nothing but a wall behind me, I turned to see what it was that peaked their interest. Well, it definitely wasn't the tarnished horse brasses, or the rather fetching, but ever-so faded watercolour. They were looking at me.

I lowered my body towards the cushioned seat and there was a noticeable, communal intake of breath. Without exception they were all looking in my direction. Surely there'd been new customers before. I couldn't believe that I was attracting so much attention. My backside made contact with the seat and I could almost taste the air as it turned sour around me.

I wasn't looking where I had placed my drink and when it landed on the table, it rocked slightly, spilling more of its contents. It wasn't resting on an even surface. I looked down to see what had caused the problem and there was a highly polished, yellow metal plaque screwed to the table top. I shifted my drink to read it.

'In memory of Sid, patron of this establishment who died right here in his favourite chair. November 17th 1989. RIP.'

Oh no! I was sat in some sort of shrine to a regular, who had passed away before I was even old enough to drink. In fact, he'd died in the very chair in which I was sat. I hoped he hadn't bled, or worse emptied his bowels and bladder as I'd heard often happens when people die. My trousers didn't feel wet, but it had been quite a number of years ago, any fluid would have dried up by now, but there was still a chance I was sat in someone else's emissions.

All these thoughts went through my head, when I remembered that the customers were still watching. One of them broke ranks and advanced in my direction. I started to rise as he reached me and he bent down and spoke.

"That's Sid's chair," he growled quietly.

"I'm sorry, I didn't..."

He interrupted, "He sat there every day since he was old enough to drink. Each morning the landlord puts out a newspaper. The first drink we all have is in Sid's memory."

"It was a mistake, I..."

He cut me off again, "So, unless you want to feel the curse of a dead man, or the boot of a living one, I suggest you get back on your feet, wipe the table, and find somewhere else to stand, or even somewhere else to drink."

I moved out from behind the table as the menacing regular backed away. I held my pint in one hand and looked around for something to wipe the table as I had been ordered to do. I was wearing a short-sleeved shirt, so I didn't even have the option of using my own clothing if I'd wanted to. I felt in my pocket and found a handkerchief. I removed it slowly to ensure that it didn't act as some sort of launcher for an acrobatic French letter. I reminded myself to move the condom to my wallet to prevent any future sudden, unwanted appearances.

The material was in no way adequate enough to soak up the amount of liquid that I had spilled, but I did my best, then placed the sodden rag back into my pocket, where the beer immediately soaked into my clothing.

I stood awkwardly in the middle of the pub trying to blend into my surroundings, but when you're a newcomer wearing a shirt and trousers in a place where the code of dress appeared to be cheap, faded tracksuits, it's impossible.

There was another empty table, this one sported a dirty dishrag and an ashtray, on which perched a half smoked cigarette. I decided against sitting at it, in case it was reserved for the ghost of the old cleaning lady, who had died of some smoking related disease.

I couldn't have felt more self conscious if I'd been naked. I stood, they stared. I didn't want them to think I was intimidated, but I was and, like dogs, they sensed my fear. I gulped at my beer trying to finish quicker, but I only succeeded in losing some of it down my shirt.

There was no way I could stay, I wanted to get out before my date arrived. I'd rather meet her outside and suggest moving to another pub, than explain the frosty reception we received at the bar, when I ordered the next round.

A couple more gulps, and some more spillage, and I carefully dropped my half empty pint glass onto the bar before heading back out to the car park. As the door closed behind me, the chatter restarted and the jukebox played again.

I'd only been outside long enough to transfer the condom to my wallet, when a taxi pulled up and Right-on climbed out. I was pleased to see that she had ditched the ankle-length skirt in favour of a pair of jeans. The trademark knee-length jumper had also gone, in favour of a thigh-length one. I wondered whether her clothes would gradually reduce in size each time we dated. Maybe, within four or five date's time she'd be wearing something that hinted at an outline of her figure.

She gave a little wave, paid the taxi driver, then walked across the car park to me. She placed her hands on my shoulders, stood on her tip-toes, and kissed me gently on the lips.

There was a faint fragrance, not a bottled scent, but a pleasant natural smell. Which is exactly what she was, natural. What this woman showed you, was exactly what you got. Except curves, she never seemed to show the curves. She didn't deviate from her strong beliefs. She had the same set of values now as she did all those years ago when I originally knew her.

You knew exactly where you stood, there was nothing false and, as a man who hadn't been altogether truthful recently, I respected that. I felt guilty. My lies were wrong and this wouldn't work if I continued with the pretence. I would build up this relationship and, when we'd become close enough to tell each other our deepest secrets, I'd confess my deceit. Hopefully she'd see the funny side, and forgive me.

She stepped back and looked at my stained shirt giving it a perfunctory wipe with the flat of her hand, as if brushing it would make it disappear.

"I tried to take a drink out of a water bottle while I was driving, and managed to spill it," I explained.

She eyed me suspiciously. "Come on then," she said. She threaded her arm through mine and started towards the pub entrance.

"Oh, we can't," I said, "there's workmen in there. It's closed for refurbishment."

"You mean workers. But I can hear music," she continued walking but I'd stopped dead, like a stubborn puppy refusing to walk any further.

"There must be the workers inside, I tried the door but it's locked."

As the words left my mouth, the front door of the pub opened and two men stepped out. When they saw me they both stopped, and continued the staring that had only been broken by my earlier departure.

"They don't look like workers," she said.

If I continued to lie, things like this were bound to happen. Either events would occur to prove me wrong, or I'd trip myself up because I'd forgotten what I'd lied about. This had to stop. She deserved better. Maybe then, in the middle of a pub car park, wasn't the right time to come clean about everything, but I conceded that I should stop adding new things for me to remember.

"I did," I sighed, "I lied."

"What? Why?"

"I've already been in the pub, I did something stupid and didn't exactly endear myself to the regulars. Part of me is too embarrassed to go back in, and another part is too scared."

"Those men are really staring at you, what did you do?"

"I may have desecrated the memory of a dead regular by sitting at the table they keep as a shrine."

She joined in what appeared to be the now national sport, and stared at me. Then she snorted and laughed. She brought her hand to her face trying to stifle the noise, but I didn't want it to stop, I liked the sound.

"So, as a result, I can't go back in there. They're all mental."

"Anger management issues," she corrected.

"Yeah, that as well."

She pointed to the front of my shirt. "Is the beer stain anything to do with it?"

"How do you know it's beer?"

"I can smell it." She laughed a bit more.

"I needed to finish my drink very quickly and get out. Unfortunately the speed of my tipping, doesn't quite match the capacity of my mouth. There was...leakage."

"Come on then, let's try somewhere else. I don't fancy watching my date get lynched."

Luckily enough her taxi hadn't yet moved away, so she guided me back towards it.

As I closed in on the car I could see that the driver was fidgeting with something in his lap. Thankfully, when I got alongside, I saw he wasn't fiddling with himself, but with a cash-loaded bumbag that sat around his waist. He looked up at me stood by his window and our eyes met.

Oh no! It was the same person who had recently robbed me.

More worryingly it was the same driver who had seen me take another woman home just a few days before. If I was lucky he wouldn't recognise me. Considering the large amount of money in his bag, he obviously fleeced hundreds of people every week, why should he remember me?

The window sank slowly into the door and the driver looked at me; this new 'stare-at-the-journalist' game had become very popular?

There was a pause before he said, "Alright mate."

Right-on moved past me, put a hand on his door and leaned down to look through the window. "Can I use you again?" she asked.

Intent on the gold medal in Olympic staring, he held my gaze for as long as he could. His eyes then flicked to her. "Course you can darling, jump in."

"Thank you, but just remember, like I said earlier, I'm not your darling."

"Whatever," he said.

We both clambered into the back and settled down. I sat behind the driver, trying to stay out of the view of his mirror. Right-on linked her arm through mine and, placing her other hand onto my bicep, she pulled herself closer to me.

The driver glanced at me through his rear view mirror. "Where to this time?" he asked.

I didn't know whether the question was aimed at me or my date. Had he remembered the last time I had used his services, or was it a reference to the journey he had taken with Right-on? Being none-the-wiser about my previous relationship with the driver, she answered, "Can you just take us to a pub that's a bit better than this?"

"No problem," and with that he started our journey.

I was on edge throughout the trip. Although there was no definite indication, I couldn't be sure that he didn't remember me. I tried not to talk during the journey as I couldn't risk the chance that he would recognise my voice, but I didn't have to worry as Right-on kept him engaged in conversation.

In answer to the eternal taxi driver questions, he was busy and he was working until midnight.

"Is this your own car?" She asked.

"Yes, love."

She bristled slightly at the term of endearment. "I'm not a 'love', I mean your family car, do you take your family in it?"

"It's my family car and my living, petal," he replied.

"I don't think I could do that, transport all sorts of people in the car that my family also use. I'm not a petal by the way."

"It's a case of necessity, sweetheart. I've got to earn a living." He was clearly using every term of endearment he could remember.

"I guess but I couldn't do it. I'd hate ferrying drunk people about. Please don't call me sweetheart."

"It's not so bad, happy drunks are fine, it's the ones that can't hold their drink that I worry about. You have to be careful with them, I don't want people being sick in my family car."

It could've been my paranoia, but I'm sure the eyes in the mirror met mine momentarily as he said it. Surely if he recognised me, and was going to say something, he'd have done it.

He took us to another little country pub and pulled up outside. Right-on opened the door and got out whilst I retrieved my wallet to pay, she moved toward the pub entrance. I handed over the cash and the driver swirled the change around in his bum-bag. He took longer than I thought necessary and I wondered whether he got a little bit of gratification out of the action.

He counted out my change which he then tipped it into my open hand.

"Don't let your bird get too pissed this time eh?" he said with a wink.

It was my turn to stare. "Thank you, but she's not a bird, she's a woman."

The taxi driver's choice of pub was a whole lot better than mine. It was more corporate, but at least the clientele weren't hostile, and there were no roped off areas to keep people off the memorial furniture.

We sat down at a cosy table in the corner and shared a few drinks. She occasionally brought up my indiscretion at the previous pub, which she found extremely amusing.

"I'm sorry I lied to you about it," I said.

"Don't worry, you're forgiven. I know why you did it."

I started to feel very guilty. Would she still be so forgiving, if she knew the full extent of my deception? It had only been a little lie, but how would a woman with her principles react to the fact that I'd been economical with the truth? I wanted to tell her that not all lies are malicious, some are made with really good intentions, so that you can get something that you really want. They're not made to hurt anyone.

I had to cut down on the lies and I really had to put her straight about my 'carnivorism'. I think I wanted it to work as a relationship.

She reached across the table and placed her hand on top of mine. "If there's anything that you'd like to talk about then we're sort of partners now, you can tell me you know," she said gently.

My mind latched onto one word. The word 'partners'. Had the woman who populated my, not-so-dry, teenage dreams just said I was her boyfriend? At no stage during those nights, when the young me wiped unrequited love off his bed sheets, did I ever think this would become a reality.

Wait! Had she asked me to tell her something? It sounded like she knew my secret, the only question was which secret?

Had she'd discovered my treachery around the vegetarianism, or the 'polygamy'? Either one wouldn't be good, but her tone of voice conveyed no anger or even disappointment; she sounded concerned.

It was then that I should've asked her to clarify what she meant so I could put her right, but whatever part of the brain that does that sort of stuff was clearly missing in my case, so I just nodded and looked thoughtful. Last time I'd misunderstood something, silence hadn't worked for me, so I'm not sure why I was relying on it to get me out of my predicament now.

She continued and I was determined to listen to every word she said. Very recently I'd failed to listen to a woman, I'd missed out on a golden opportunity and it wouldn't happen again. I was ready to hear, and accept, any offer especially if it included sex.

"It's not something that you should be embarrassed about you know, it happens to men."

I'd had conversations that started like this before, but usually neither party was clothed, or at least one of us was a doctor.

"You have to be really careful, you can't keep doing it. You can make yourself seriously ill," she said.

Yes, the doctor had said that once too.

It was official, I had no idea what the hell she was talking about. I was pretty sure that she wasn't worried about my pretend vegetarianism, or even my lack of ability to date just one woman. As far as I'm aware, neither of those came with medical complications.

"You don't need to hide it, it's something we can sort together."

She knew I was lying about something, unfortunately I didn't know what she knew, so I didn't want to confess to something that she didn't know about.

"Lots of people have eating disorders, it's nothing to be frightened of."

What? Was this another of her crazy Right-on ideas? Being a meat eater was now an 'eating disorder'. Typical hippy, just because something didn't fit her own cock-eyed view of the universe, she'd labelled it as a mental illness. Honestly, the nerve of some people.

She increased the pressure of her hold on my hand. She was no match for God-groupie where grip was concerned, but then protein was missing from her diet. "I'm guessing you're wondering how I knew," she said.

As a matter of fact the thought hadn't even crossed my mind. I was basically a compulsive liar and there is no way anyone could have kept a tab on the untruths I'd told, I was bound to trip up at some stage. I was actually surprised that it had taken this long.

She cupped both her hands over the top of mine. "Do you remember when you were at my house and you spilt that drink down your trousers?"

Technically she had knocked the drink down me, but I didn't want to argue. I needed to know where this conversation was headed.

"Yes."

"Well, a little while after you'd left, I went to the bathroom and I found something that worried me a bit."

I must have looked confused but she continued. "My toilet doesn't flush properly, you left some remnants of vomit in the bowl. It doesn't take a detective to work it out. I didn't want to say anything but if this relationship is going to work then we need to be open."

With everything that had gone off in my life I'd forgotten I'd left the contents of my dinner in the unflushable toilet. The game was up. Maybe it was time to admit my duplicity. Not only had I lied about being a vegetarian, I couldn't even stomach the home cooked meal that she had lovingly prepared. I hadn't even been brave enough to tell her that it had consisted of everything that I found repulsive in the culinary world.

It was nothing to do with her morals, she believed that I suffered from some sort of genuine eating disorder. The detective in her should have also noticed that someone who suffered with such a disorder would probably be carrying slightly less weight than I did.

What she had seen had gone directly from plate to the toilet, with a slight stop in the fold of my t-shirt along the way, but the stuff that had bobbed around in the bowl had been nowhere a digestive system. I concede, it may have been mashed slightly by being stabbed with a toilet brush, but she was basically comparing what she had cooked, to vomit.

"I'm so sorry." I raised the hand that wasn't being comforted to my mouth and rubbed my lips. I lowered my gaze from her eyes to the table. "I feel like such an idiot."

So many times previously my mind had failed me at such crucial points in conversations, and I had ended up in situations that, had I told the truth, could've been avoided. Each time I reasoned that I should have come clean, or point out that someone was mistaken, something diverted my attention and my mouth worked independently of my brain.

She gave my hand another reassuring squeeze. "Look it's ok, you can talk to me you know. I'm not going to judge you."

Which I found ironic, as she constantly judged people by correcting what they said. I had to learn to moderate my own language to be more politically correct. And I found her ethics hard work. I'm all for protecting the environment but I don't want to have to sacrifice the things I liked, or indeed loved. Leather shoes, good coffee, fine wine, and of course meat. I didn't want to give any of it up.

She had been the object of my desires for all my school years. For reasons I hadn't managed to work out I found myself dating her; something my teenage self would never have believed could happen. I still liked her, but if we had any chance of succeeding as a couple then I would have to change, or she would have to accept me for what I was; a wine-drinking, coffee loving, carnivore, with shoes made from the bit of the cow I couldn't eat.

She bent her head sightly and tried to look into my eyes, perhaps she saw the battle that raged inside my head.

"Are you ok?" she asked.

I nodded and took the deep breath I needed to break the news.

With her free hand she cupped my chin and raised my head so that she looked straight into my eyes. I looked back, those beautiful sparkling eyes contained a hint of sadness. I had misled her and she didn't deserve that.

She leaned across the table and kissed me, pressing her lips home gently. She held the position for a few seconds. My brain quickly compared it to the snog I'd received from Hamster-chick. Her's had been hard, sloppy, invasive, and most of all came with the added danger of immolation. There was no competition, Right-on was the hands-down winner.

Perhaps now would be the time to start to put things right. I had written off two potential girlfriends and Right-on was the only remaining contender for the coveted position. I didn't want to see her slip through my fingers just because I'd been an ass. She may have had some strange ideas and beliefs but she was right about one thing, if we were to work as a couple, we needed to be open.

I took a deep breath, "I've not got an eating disorder," I paused, "I was just unwell that day. You'd gone to a lot of effort cooking and I didn't want you to think that I was ungrateful by not eating, or not even turning up."

Baby steps.

The path to truthfulness is a long one. You can't just blurt out that you're a liar, people will think that nothing you say can ever be trusted. I needed to approach it slowly and not drop all the bombshells in one go.

"I'm sorry, I should have said something," I apologised.

"It does explain why you brought the date to such a sharp end, I was kind of hoping we could have taken things a little further."

My stomach flipped and I recognised that it was one of those points where my mouth usually made up something in order to get what I wanted. I wasn't going to let it happen again.

- NINETEEN -

The taxi ride back to her house was uneventful, thankfully the driver didn't know me and I didn't do anything to change that.

Right-on waited at the side of the car whilst I paid the driver. When I'd done, she linked her arm through mine and we walked up the path.

"So, are you staying for that coffee we didn't have on our first date?"

Not if it's that goddamn awful stuff you served me last time.

"As long as you don't tip it into my lap," I said.

"Well, let's make a deal. If I do spill it on you, then I promise to wipe you down properly." She gave me a little wink.

"Deal," I said, and held out my hand, she shook it.

As we stepped through the doorway into the hall, I was thinking how best to orchestrate a spillage when it became apparent that I wouldn't have to. She closed the door, then turned and placed another one of those kisses on my lips, and this time I returned it.

It was passionate and not harsh. There was no tugging at clothes, or a hurried need to get undressed. Our lips parted and she took my hand, leading me along the hallway and up the stairs which, unless she had kept the contents of the toilet to show me, could only mean one thing. She guided me across the small landing past the bathroom, where she had incorrectly diagnosed my illness, and into her bedroom.

If I'd been asked, I could probably have described the room before I saw it. It was similar in colour to the lounge. Dark reds and browns, with thin, wispy material draped over various surfaces. The same material was twisted around a pole above the window in an effort to imitate curtains. They were no use in stopping daylight, or curious eyes, from penetrating. I made a mental note not to walk past it naked with the lights on.

Naked! Oh God, it was going to happen. I was about to have sex with her. I wanted to invent a time machine to travel back and tell the teenage me to hang in there, and that all those wasted tissues wouldn't be in vain.

She removed her jumper and put both her arms around my neck. She pulled me in to her and kissed me again. It was at that point that I was thankful I'd had a very long shower, and that I'd paid particular attention to those parts that were about to be exposed to someone other than me. I'd put on my best underwear, it wasn't that I'd expected them to be seen by another person, I just wasn't prepared to risk it and wear an old, holey pair which might prove an immediate passion-killer. I quickly turned my attention to my left buttock, to see if I could feel my wallet pressed against it. I was pretty sure it was there, which meant that so was my faithful condom.

The condom that was nearly lost in action at the meal with God-groupie's family. The condom that, if I'd listened properly, would more than likely have been used in first time sex with a very 'nice' woman. The condom that was about to fulfil its destiny.

All my thinking meant that I'd been inert for a few seconds. My brain reminded me to pay attention, we were at 'Def Com 5' and all senses needed to be on high alert. I rejoined her in the kissing, and concentrated on feeling good about that specific moment in time.

We ran our arms up and down each others backs. I wasn't sure whether I should be stroking her buttocks, or making an attempt to undo her bra through her t-shirt. Would it be bad form if I unfastened a bra without first taking off the outer clothing, or was that a cool thing to do? Should I wait until she'd taken the t-shirt off.

My brain butted in. *For God's sake man, pay attention and just go with it.* I needed to up my game, the woman meant business.

Her tongue quickly darted in and out of my mouth. It was extremely sensual and I tried to do the same but it felt unnatural, like I was trying to clean the remnants out of an empty yoghurt pot.

I was reminded of Hamster-chick's attempts to cram her tongue into my mouth and there was a fleeting memory of all the associated tastes and smells.

Ahem, you're pre-foreplay, perhaps you should be paying more than a passing interest.

I tried the tongue thing again, whilst I attempted to coordinate my hands on her back. I was convinced I wasn't doing any of it right. Maybe I should just let her take the lead. She'd clearly done it before.

It hit me suddenly, I'd not previously thought that she may have had other lovers. What if they had been better than me? What if my performance was a disaster? I wasn't that experienced with women, but I'd never had one tell me I was a disappointment, but then again none of them had ever congratulated me either! The Tin-man had left me for someone else, she'd never given a reason, maybe I'd been dreadful in bed.

I thanked my brain. In my first sexual encounter since being dumped by my fiancée, it had dredged up thoughts that I'd resigned to the pit of my brain. I pushed away the emerging memories of my previous sex life before it could drop anchor into my grey matter.

I must've been giving off some sort of external signal that all was not well, because Right-on pulled back to look at me, she kept her hands linked behind my neck.

"Everything ok?" she asked.

I nodded. "Absolutely perfect."

"You look a bit sad."

I shook my head. "No I'm fine."

"Ah well, just in case you're a little unhappy, I know something that might cheer you up." She let go of me, took hold of the hem of her t-shirt, pulled it slowly over her head, and then dropped it on the floor. It was the most sensual thing I've ever seen.

Underneath her top was a white, lacy bra with a floral design.

The curves that she kept so expertly hidden were incredible. She wasn't finished, she popped the button on the front of her jeans and pulled both parts of the waistband with enough force to free the other buttons. She pushed them down over her hips and then shimmied until the jeans hit the floor where she stepped out of them.

I had no idea what my expression was, but my mouth was probably open in a wide smile, with my teeth showing. It was likely that a sliver of drool was hanging from my bottom lip. Whatever it was, there is no way it was attractive to the opposite sex, but it didn't seem to concern her.

She was wearing a pair of white pants that were the exact same design as the bra. Someone had once told me that if a woman's bra and pants matched, then it was her decision to have sex not yours. Who was it that told me that? Oh yes, the Receptionist. Not only was she quite astute, she was more than willing to share her knowledge and her experiences. Well, I definitely had something to tell her when we next met.

Listen mate, until you put your mind to the job in hand, I'm taking no further part in this activity. Wake me if you need me.

It wasn't the brain talking this time. I realised that the organ that had the most to gain, was no longer participating in the game.

She stood in front of me, her nakedness covered by the thinnest of material. She had taken the initiative, it was every man's dream, but for some reason although the rudder was free, the engine room wasn't working. It was because I hadn't concentrated on what was happening in front of me, I had allowed my mind to wander. I told myself she was a beautiful woman, the object of my desires, and the subject of many a fantasy. She was, as near as dammit, naked less than two feet in front of me. If it was going to happen then I needed the cooperation of all my bits.

I stared at her. I examined her eyes, her lips, and the way her hair rested on her shoulders. The smooth curves were complemented by a toned body that she kept hidden under all manner of baggy clothes. She had undressed and it was a certainty that, within a short space of time, this was going to turn into a sexual olympics...and I'd forgotten to pack any working equipment. I'd read somewhere that this exclusively male problem was made worse the more stressed you became. To combat it, I had to forget it was happening and just go with the flow.

She placed one hand on her hip and cocked her head to one side. "Your turn," she said, and nodded in my direction.

She wanted me in my underwear too. I'm not sure why I was so surprised, after all, nakedness is a pre-requisite for the sex thing. I couldn't match her toned physique. There was no doubt that she would be massively disappointed when I took my shirt off, but nowhere near as disappointed as she be would once I'd removed my trousers.

I was right, I would have something to tell the Receptionist. I pictured her wiping the corner of her eyes delicately, because she was laughing so much at my predicament.

I felt a pang and a slight churn in my stomach not dissimilar to butterflies. Thank God the engine had started, I'd finally taken my situation seriously and the little athlete had answered the call to compete.

The largest ever dose of self-consciousness injected itself firmly in my mind as I unbuttoned my shirt. I slid it off my shoulders and stood topless. I checked her face for signs that she felt let down. She smiled, was it happiness or pity? Whilst I looked at a vision of beauty, she was faced with the Michelin man's slightly less chubby, younger brother. There was no guessing what was going through her mind?

I realised that the stirring little Olympian had retreated again. What the hell! Didn't he realise he was needed for competition. All those hours I'd spent with him in training, preparing him for just such an occasion, were wasted. I needed his participation and at that point, I'd even settle for him jumping the gun.

I unfastened my belt and slowly pulled it through the loops in my trousers. I needed to buy myself some time to get back on track.

What more stimulation does an athlete need to participate? He was one of the main players in a major event and he didn't seem interested in getting started. He needed some encouragement. I tried to think what it was that had caused the reaction a short time earlier.

She'd kissed me, she'd done a little strip-tease, my mind had wandered, about a million other thoughts had squeezed their way into my mind while she'd been stood in front of me. It was clear that relaxing and letting nature take its course was not going to happen, so I wracked my brain for the thought that had caused the stirring.

My de-robing took a painfully long time, she'd either think that it was some excruciatingly slow strip-tease, or that I was retarded. If I had been in her shoes I'd have guessed the latter. I slowly unfastened my fly, one button at a time.

Would this have happened with God-groupie? Because I hadn't been listening I didn't give myself the chance to find out. I began to wonder whether I had some sort of attention deficit disorder. I was on the verge of a sexual encounter with another woman, and I couldn't even give her my complete concentration.

Would I share this disaster with the Receptionist? It was an extremely personal thing, perhaps I'd lie to her about it and say everything went like a dream. On the other hand, I'd never lied to her about anything, so may be I should tell her. I pictured her sat on a swivel chair with her feet on a desk as she tapped away on her mobile phone. I was two buttons into the undoing of my trousers when I felt it again. There was a shudder in my stomach and a little bit of electricity skipped through my veins.

Bloody hell! The Receptionist! The thought of her is what had fired the starting gun. Despite the fact that an attractive woman was stood in front of me, partially naked, and I was on the verge of having sex with her, the thing that had caused any reaction were thoughts of another woman.

Confusion flooded my mind. I needed some thinking time.

"Can I use the bathroom," I asked.

Her eyes widened in surprise and a look of disbelief dashed across her face. She recovered quickly and pointed at the bed. "Ok, I'll be right here."

I bent and picked up my shirt and belt and headed for the door.

"Use the one off the kitchen, the one up here is still blocked," she called after me. If she thought it was strange that I'd picked up my clothing, she didn't say anything.

Hold on, there as a toilet on the ground floor, and it had a working flush? If I'd known that on Sunday, it might just have saved me a whole lot of embarrassment.

Clutching my clothing, I walked quickly down the stairs completely forgetting the fact that I'd removed my belt, and un-buttoned my trousers. Unfortunately gravity didn't have such a poor memory. In the blink of a eye, my loose trousers slipped down to my knees.

My brain hadn't registered what had happened so there was no message to the legs to tell them to stop. They continued their movement, my ankles restricted by the waistband of my trousers. This restriction was my literal downfall. The front leg tried to reach the next step down, but it might as well have been shackled to the other one. Before the foot had found a safe landing on the next stair, it dragged its partner off the previous step and for a split second no part of me was in touch with the ground; then at some point during my accelerated descent, every part of me was in touch with the stairs.

I landed in the hallway in a crumpled heap. I did a quick system analysis and, although I hurt in a number of places, I was pretty sure that nothing was broken.

"Are you ok?" came the shout from somewhere above my launchpad.

"Yes," I replied, "just took a slight tumble. I'm fine."

"Did you miss a step?" she called.

No I hit every single one. "Yes, it's ok, I'm ok, everything is ok."

I noticed that she hadn't rushed to my aid. Perhaps she was

concerned about the possibility of me bleeding, and being a vegan she wasn't allowed to deal with it, or maybe she was naked and didn't want to walk past the inadequately covered window.

I clambered to my feet and pulled up my trousers. I secured them with the buttons, and then gathered the clothing that I had jettisoned into the air when I had performed the unscheduled, indoor free-fall.

I tried to shake off the few pains I had and walked to the kitchen. I flicked the switch and light flooded the room. There was only one possible option for the bathroom, so I opened the door that I had initially thought was a pantry. The dangling light cord swayed as I yanked it to put the light on. It was a small space that comprised of a toilet and a basin. I was momentarily concerned about the hygiene implications of having a toilet so close to a food preparation area, but I had other things to worry about.

I closed the door behind me and dropped the clothing I was carrying onto the floor. The closed toilet seat groaned as I sat down on it. I put my head in my hands and screwed my eyes tight shut. Just maybe it was a really bad dream and any moment I would wake up with nothing but a fading memory.

It was a surreal enough experience to have been a figment of my own imagination, for a start I'd been within a whisker of having sex, and that never happened in real life. I told myself to wake up several times. After a few minutes I opened my eyes and I was still sat in a small toilet, wearing half of my clothes with the rest on the floor at my feet. It was real.

There was no ambiguity in this situation, a beautiful woman had kissed me and performed a partial strip-tease. For once I hadn't misread the signs, everything had been cantering along quite well, but there had been a refusal by one of the main participants, which had meant that I'd had to bring the proceedings to a halt. What the hell was wrong with me?

Slowly, the feeling of pain broke through. I rubbed my left arm and realised that it was sore where the friction of my fall had exposed some raw skin. It was sticky and I winced as I touched it gingerly with my fingers. A carpet burn, how appropriate. Maybe I could still convince the Receptionist that my night had been one of spectacular sex.

The Receptionist! I thought about her again, but I was also thinking about telling more lies. That was my problem, my desire to impress people meant that I lied because I thought it made me more attractive to the opposite sex. I was so insecure that I didn't think women would be interested in me, so I made things up.

I needed to find someone who accepted me for who I was, the 36-year-old, meat-eating, religious sceptic. It was time I stopped lying.

Over the last few months I'd done nothing but make my own life hard work. I'd told lies, I'd embarrassed myself, I'd taken drugs, and I'd even fallen foul of the law. If I was honest with myself, and it was about time I should be, I felt awful for having behaved the way I had.

As I stared at the toilet floor, I did a mental audit of my current situation.

Not so long ago, I'd had three girlfriends. I had juggled them successfully for a short period of time, and none of them knew of my deceit. Whilst this didn't make what I'd done any better, it did mean that as they didn't know I'd cheated, I'd at least saved them from some pain. Although I'm suggesting that they would have been upset, and not relieved, or homicidally angry.

I still struggled with the concept of when commitment actually kicks into a relationship. Is it as soon as you start seeing each other? After the first kiss? The moment you declare yourself a couple? Or maybe the first sexual experience? I had no idea, but if I'd been seeing just one of them, then there'd have probably been some sort of monogamous expectation on my behalf, so there was no excuse for it not working the other way.

There was no doubt, I was a bad person.

Hamster-chick had been a mistake. Even if I'd not lied, it wouldn't have worked. I could not have kept up with her lifestyle. I'd have been dead by my 40th birthday, which would be more tragic to her as she'd think I was only 30. Could I have tamed her? Maybe, but it would've taken a couple of years, and who am I to change someone who so obviously enjoyed her life?

Like I've said before, I'd enjoyed God-groupie's company, she was a 'nice' person. She was serious about us. The relationship, if that's what I wanted to call it, had accelerated faster than an impotent, half naked-journalist hurtling down a set of stairs. I wasn't comfortable with it, and that told me it wasn't meant to be.

Then there was Right-on, who at this very moment was less that 15 vertical feet away and probably naked. I lifted my face and looked to the ceiling as if I might be able to see her. It was only sex for God's sake. Why the hell couldn't I just get on with it? Perhaps I didn't fancy her? Who was I kidding? Of course I fancied her, I always had done. Which made the situation all the more confusing.

And finally the Receptionist. An unexpected factor in my relationship dilemma. We'd flirted and shared our experiences, well I'd shared mine, she'd hinted at her's. Other than the odd brush past and cheeky slap, there been very little in the way of physical contact. Why was it that she had poked her way into my thoughts? I started to think about the messages she'd sent when I'd been on dates. Could they have been done on purpose? Had she attempted to sabotage my chances? Surely she knew that I was quite capable of sabotaging my own love life.

I analysed the messages and conversations we'd had, and I started to read things into them, things that possibly weren't there. I'd never asked her out and I wasn't sure why. I'd lied to make myself seem more dynamic, but she knew the real me, she knew I was dull. There was no way she'd be interested.

But I had to find out. I had to speak to her.

I pulled my phone from my pocket. There were two messages waiting for me, both from the Receptionist. I opened the first one:

How's it going?

It had been sent a couple of hours before. The second had arrived less than 30 minutes ago.

I guess you're tied up and can't talk. Speak soon. X

For some reason, I honed in on the kiss at the end of the text. It had a new meaning now.

I replied:

I've hit an all time low. Need to talk. See you tomorrow.

It seemed like I'd only just hit the 'send' button when the phone buzzed with her reply. I remembered how her fingers zipped across the screen of her phone.

Sounds interesting. Looking forward to it. X

There it was again, a little kiss.

I had to break the news to Right-on; I know you're on your bed in all your naked loveliness expecting me to perform all sorts of sexual gymnastics, but I'm afraid my parallel bar isn't quite up to it, as I've just realised it's quite possible I fancy someone else.

Maybe that wasn't the way to break the news to her. Perhaps if I told her I suffered from some sort of genetic erectile dysfunction that could not be cured, and it wouldn't be fair on her to live a sexless life. Or perhaps she'd believe that I was gay, that would solve all my problems, with the added bonus that it would perfectly align with her political correctness.

Wait! I was doing it again. Faced with a problem my first reaction was to lie. I slammed my fist on my knee and caught the raw skin under my jeans.

This was going to stop! I intended to go upstairs and explain the situation to her truthfully.

- TWENTY -

You thought I'd bottle it didn't you? Well, that makes two of us. I have to admit that the thought did cross my mind.

I can't say it was easy, it was probably one of the hardest things I've ever had to do. I told her that the whole thing didn't feel right, and I wasn't going to have sex just for the sake of it. I said I didn't want her to feel used when the relationship didn't go anywhere.

There was no crying, just a lot on understanding nods and hugs. It made me feel even worse. I would have preferred it if she'd screamed and shouted and thrown some heavy object at me that had been carved by a blind, limbless, Peruvian Grandmother. I wanted more of a reaction, but perhaps I'm not as good a catch as I'd like to think.

I didn't mention anything about having feelings for another woman, that wouldn't have been fair. Maybe I was learning when withholding the truth was the right thing to do.

I'd had relationships in the past and things have gone wrong and a lot of the time it had been my fault, but this was not my finest hour. Although I knew I had made the right decision, I felt absolutely terrible the next day and have to admit to not sleeping properly, if at all.

So, after a period of time where I'd had the attention of three women, I found myself bereft of female companionship. How the hell can a man go out with three women and not have sex with any of them? Well, it's not easy, you have to be a special kind of stupid.

I'd fallen into the three relationships and I needed to do something that I'd never done before, I needed to make a plan. I couldn't remember when I'd last initiated contact with a woman with the intention of asking her out on a date. Although I'd never thought of the Receptionist as a friend, she wasn't a stranger, which should have made it easier.

They say familiarity breeds contempt. I'm not sure who 'they' are, but 'they' are wrong. In these circumstances, familiarity bred a kind of confusion. I knew her, there was no need to break the ice, I didn't going into the situation cold, but I wasn't entirely sure what to say. She knew I was a liar and that I'd been trialling three different women as potential girlfriends. She knew there'd been no sex, but my actions were surely evidence that I couldn't be trusted to stay monogamous. That was my problem; how to make someone who knows all your secrets actually think you're worth their time.

I played out every scenario in my head. From the one where she swooned into my arms and I carried her out of the office to a new life, to the one where I was on my knees begging and she's laughing uncontrollably. The reality would be more towards the second version.

In the end I decided that I'd go to the office and wait for an opportunity. There would be some sort of innuendo in the conversation at some stage, and I would exploit that.

Bearing in mind that I had recently turned up to work in clothes I'd been wearing for more than 24 hours and smelling of vomit, I made sure that I took advantage of my lack of sleep by getting out of bed early and paid particular attention to my personal grooming. This was a woman who had seen me in every phase of my cleanliness so I thought I should make an effort.

I didn't want to appear too eager to speak to her, so I sat at home far longer than I wanted. When I say 'sat', I mean thinking, pacing, and worrying.

Although it was something I'd done a hundred times before, when I walked into the office, I felt more awkward than I had ever done. I tried desperately to look casual which just made me feel as though I was walking like Bambi in high-heels. I'd never felt so conspicuous. People looked up from their desks as I tottered by, they probably always did this, but this time it was as though they could see my awkwardness.

My heart pounded against my rib cage and my breathing quickened. Then I saw it...her empty chair, she wasn't there! I looked around in an exaggerated nonchalant way. It was so nonchalant that it would've looked desperate to anyone watching. She wasn't sat at any of the other desks. I felt a sudden stab of panic. It wasn't one of my scenarios. I'd psyched myself up, I had a plan, not much of a plan admittedly, but I hadn't even entertained the fact that she wouldn't be there.

People would have asked questions if I'd turned around and walked straight out, so I dumped myself into a chair, pressed the power button on a computer and waited it for boot up. I was through the sinking feeling and now at rock bottom. Why had she not thought to mention not being at work when I sent the text? Why should she? We weren't close. I didn't mean that much to her. I was that creepy weirdo who turned up in her office every so often with sordid tales of his miserable love life.

The computer sang into life and I stared at the screen. I had nothing to write. There was nothing to submit. I had turned up for the sole purpose of seeing her, and she wasn't there. I was conscious that others might be watching me, so I pulled a notebook from my pocket and started flicking through the pages.

I checked my phone again, just in case I'd missed a message. Nothing.

Obviously she'd taken the day off to spend time with her boyfriend or girlfriend, or both. Another pang jabbed me but I knew what it was, it was jealousy. How could I have been so blind all that time?

The computer was still thinking whether it was going to work for me when I felt a hand on my shoulder and the closeness of a body behind me. A mug appeared in front of me and 'thocked' onto the desk.

"Coffee, two," said the Receptionist.

"Th..thanks," I stuttered.

"Let me look at you," she said. She grabbed the arm of my chair and swivelled it so I was facing her. She perched herself on the edge of the desk, right next to me and made a show of looking me up and down; she shook her head, "Nope," she said.

"No, what?" I asked.

"No, you didn't have sex last night, or at least you don't look like a man who had sex last night. Unless of course it was the worst experience of your life. That might explain your slightly disappointed look."

"Well, I've had worse experiences," I said.

"Really?"

I sighed. "Actually, no I haven't. Last night was the single most difficult experience I've had since…well, since ever."

She shifted her weight backwards, so that she was now sat on the desk, and crossed her legs.

"Oh, do tell."

I sighed. "The abridged version involves a quick beer and an invite for a coffee that never got made. It was followed by near-nakedness, a failure to pay attention to the situation, confusion, and a subsequent forward roll down a flight of stairs. It ended with hugs and empty promises to remain friends."

"The only two parts I'm really interested in are the nakedness and the forward roll. Now tell me, were you naked during the forward roll?'"

I nodded. "Partially, and I have the bruises to prove it."

She burst into laughter and placed her hand on my arm as if to stop herself from falling off the desk. When the laughing subsided, she hadn't removed her hand. It felt hot, the heat worked its way up to my face, and I blushed.

"So was the forward roll before, during, or after sex?" she asked.

"Instead of."

She took her hand off my arm. "Strange idea, I usually substitute ice cream and chocolate."

I shook my head as I relived the experience, or more accurately the reason it had ended. Several hours before, it had seemed so obvious and easy. I had feelings for the Receptionist, and I just needed to tell her.

"So why the gymnastics and not sex?" she asked.

I had practiced this interaction over and over again before I'd turned up at the office, but as soon as I got there I lost all power of rational thought. The back of my neck prickled uncomfortably and heat flushed through me. I wasn't sure how to say that thoughts of her had short-circuited my brain, and sabotaged any chance I had of performing in the bedroom.

"It just didn't feel right," I said.

"In what way?"

"I'm not sure. I was stood in front of a partially naked woman and everything indicated that it was going to be a night to remember, but the thought of sex with her just didn't seem right," I shrugged.

"I'm sorry...does not...compute,' she said in a robotic voice. "So you ran away so fast you fell down stairs whilst unclothed?"

That about summed it up. In fact it just about summed up my life. When anything went wrong I ran away and, more often than not, I tripped myself up, both literally and metaphorically. "It's difficult to explain, something stopped me before I got too involved."

It was her turn to shake her head. "I'm sorry, it doesn't make sense. You've been trialling women for the part of your girlfriend, and one of them pulls out all the stops for the audition she knows nothing about, and still you're not satisfied. Have you ever thought you might be very difficult to please?"

"It's not easy to be pleased when you don't know what you want in the first place."

My brain was shouting at me to tell her how I felt. I couldn't understand why I was so hesitant to say anything. All I had to do was ask her out for a drink.

"Well, what is it you want?" she asked.

I knew exactly what I wanted. I wanted her and the conversation had presented the perfect opportunity to confess how I felt; to tell her that I'd been completely blind to what was directly in front of me. It was time to see if she was willing to take a chance on a loser like me. It was a 'now or never' situation.

Then my phone rang.

"You don't get away without answering my question," she said sternly, wagging her finger.

She watched as I fished my phone out of my pocket. The ringing number flashed on the display, but because it wasn't saved in the phone's memory it didn't have an accompanying name. Unfortunately, although the phone might not have recognised it, I did. The Tin-man was calling me.

My heart was still trying to come to terms with the rhythmic work-out it had done whilst I wrestled with my romantic incompetence. It caught its foot on the rope it had been using to skip. I was simultaneously scared, intrigued, and excited. There'd been no contact since the split; even when I tried to sort out the cancellation of wedding arrangements, my call had been screened out by the Geordie usurper.

She'd gone away without a word of explanation. Then, just as I was plucking up the courage to tell another woman I had feelings for her, she wanted to talk. Her timing was impeccable. I hesitated and stared at the screen.

"Not answering it?" asked the Receptionist.

"Erm, I'm not sure,' I said.

"Is it one of the women you're avoiding?"

"Sort of."

"Oh, which one?"

"My ex-fiancee!"

Her big brown eyes widened and her mouth opened in surprise. She quickly regained her composure, "Don't even think about answering it!" she warned.

Although part of me still held a grudge, somewhere inside I desperately wanted to hear her voice. I had to make a decision, and quickly, it was only a few more rings before the answer machine would kick in.

The Receptionist dived forwards and made a grab for the phone. "End the call, don't speak to her." She was serious.

I twisted away from her so she couldn't reach my outstretched hand, at the same time trying to put my own thoughts into some sort of order. I had convinced myself that I was over her, but the simple ring of a phone had thrown that conviction into doubt. My mind raced.

The phone was about to divert to the machine so I stabbed the 'answer' button with my finger and connected the call.

The Receptionist reached around me and tried to grab my hand. I held her at arms length and raised the phone to my ear. When she saw me do this, she backed off. She shook her finger at me again and mouthed the words, "Hang up'. I turned and legged it out of the office door, until I was stood on my own.

"Hello?" I said tentatively.

"Hi," said the voice that I had wanted to hear for so long.

There was an awkward pause.

"How have you been?" she asked.

What a stupid question! You dumped me, you ran off with someone. You abandoned me. I had to cancel the wedding. You left without so much as a 'goodbye'. I had no idea what I'd done wrong. Why did you run into the arms of another man? My life has run out of control and I've done so many stupid things.

"Fine," I said, "and you?"

"Ok, I guess. We need to talk."

Now you want to talk. I was over you. I thought I was anyway. You can't just call after all this time. Do you realise how upset I've been? Do you know how angry you made me? You can't expect me to be civil.

"Ok," I replied.

"I think I owe you an apology, what I did was wrong,' she spoke quietly.

It wasn't just wrong. You cannot begin to understand the hurt you have caused me. You left me alone without an explanation, just a phone call to say it was over. What you did was heartless.

"You must've had your reasons," I said.

"I've had lots of time to think, and leaving you was a mistake. We need to talk?'

Talk! About what? About how I cried myself to sleep every

night for a week? How I struggled to sleep for days because every time I closed my eyes I saw your face? How everything around the house reminds me of you?

"Ok."

"Can we meet up?" she asked.

You don't get to do this. You can't just ring me up like you didn't tear my heart right out of my chest. You can't expect me to be at your beck and call; to just drop everything and come running back just because you ask.

"Yes, sure."

- TWENTY ONE -

It was two days since the unexpected phone call and I found myself sat waiting nervously in a coffee shop.

I'd prepared myself all day. I'd woke early and cleaned the house from top to bottom. There was no indication that she would come back but if she did, I wanted to make sure it didn't look like I'd fallen apart whilst living on my own.

Once the house was tidy, I'd turned my attention to me. I was washed, brushed, scrubbed, and clean shaven.

Clothes-wise, I wanted to make an impression. I went out shopping and brought something new. It wasn't anything special. I wanted to look fresh. She probably thought I was a loser, so being well-groomed made me feel confident.

You never get a second chance to make a first impression, but at least I had a chance to make a better one.

To say I was apprehensive would be an understatement. I had feelings for her, but I wasn't sure whether they were reciprocated. Today was important to discover whether she felt anything other than pity. After everything that had happened, I wanted to be sure about how I felt.

Before I'd been dumped, life had been predictable. I went to work, I came home, I spent time with my fiancee. Like my brother had said, I'd become an old married man well before my time.

Life had become complicated since the break-up. I'd made so many mistakes. My relationship had finished and I'd crumbled and been weak. I'd let myself be led by my own stupidity. My ego was boosted by having had the attention of three women. My behaviour had been unacceptable, but my life had been far from dull.

There'd been three women in my life, one was morally good but pretentious.

The second was a maniac. She drank too much and spent her life in a kind of limbo, she lived from one selfish experience to another, without a thought for the others around her. We had that much in common but nothing else.

The last one; nice but too eager. She committed to a relationship too early and that frightened me.

I'd been in denial since I'd found myself unexpectedly single. My misery had been buried and on the occasion it had surfaced, I had pushed it back down and carried on. I had refused to face it head-on.

Well, the time had come. What I was about to do was definitely the right thing. I knew where I was headed, I just needed to get my life back on track.

Steam climbed from the frothy head of the large cup of coffee in front of me. I'd sat with my back to the door and each time I heard the door open, I resisted the urge to turn and have a look. If she came in and saw me, I wanted her to have the opportunity to change her mind and walk away. I wouldn't have held it against her either, I'd have completely understood.

We both had to be sure it was what we wanted. I checked my phone more out of habit than expectation. There was a single message.

Almost with you. X

I caught my breath and felt my heart quicken. I'd thought about what I'd do when I saw her. Should I kiss her, and if I did should it be on the cheek or on the lips? I wasn't sure whether a hug would be too much physical contact.

I was so lost in my thoughts that I didn't hear the door open, so I was taken by surprise when two hands came from behind me and covered my eyes.

"Guess who?" said a voice.

"It could be anyone," I replied.

The soft hands left my eyes and I turned around.

"Number four reporting for duty sir," said the Receptionist, and she planted a kiss on my lips.

- TWENTY TWO -

As I opened my front door, I stepped into the hallway, bent down and picked up the small pile of letters that rested on the doormat. I dropped my keys onto the small table that had once sported a landline telephone, before that sort of thing had become obsolete. The table had become a dumping ground for small change and keys.

"I take it the kitchen is this way?" said the Receptionist as she walked past me clutching a bottle of wine by its neck.

"Yes," I pointed to the kitchen door, "I'll just sort this and I'll be with you." I was sifting through the mail and resigning anything that looked slightly unwanted onto the table beside my keys.

Having spent the whole afternoon in the coffee shop, we'd decided to grab some take-away food. I'd enjoyed her company and didn't want to see her leave. It had been civilised, but fun. We talked and laughed, mainly about my misadventures during the previous weeks. I filled her in on some of the things that I hadn't told her, which wasn't much.

It was casual and relaxed. I didn't have to worry about being something I wasn't. For once I could just enjoy someone's company and be myself.

When she suggested grabbing some food and carrying on our date at my house. I'd agreed, and not because I thought it might lead to intimacy, but because I didn't want the date to end.

I followed her into the kitchen holding two envelopes that had passed the junk mail test. She was clattering about in the cupboards retrieving plates. She moved around like she'd been here a thousand times before.

"Are those the right ones?" she asked, pointing to two wine

glasses that she had fetched from a cupboard and placed on the kitchen side.

"They're the only ones," I said.

I couldn't help but think how right she looked, busying herself in my kitchen.

"Anything interesting?" She nodding towards the post in my hand.

I looked at the envelopes, having almost forgotten I had them, "I don't know."

"Well, open them then."

I picked the stiffer of the two envelopes and slid my finger into the gap at the top and tore it open. It was a card. Every year, the birthday card from my brother was late. It could be days or, as in this case, weeks. He blamed his busy lifestyle and always had an excuse; work, travel, Beelzebub's dance competitions, Lucifer's piano recitals, the dog's castration. There was always some excuse, but I didn't mind.

"Cutlery?" said the Receptionist.

"Drawer, next to the sink." I indicated behind me.

She squeezed past and as she did she stopped and kissed me on the cheek. It was quick, soft, and gentle.

I pulled the card from its envelope. There was a cartoon of a man wearing a shirt and sleeveless sweater, holding a cup of tea. The wording said: '*Brother, For your birthday I wanted to get you something that you so desperately needed...*'

I opened the card:

'*...but how do you wrap a life?*'

If only he knew!

Printed in Great
Britain
by Amazon